FALSE FUTURE

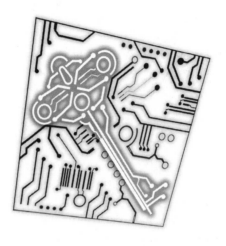

FALSE FUTURE

DAN KROKOS

Hyperion

Los Angeles   New York

Copyright © 2014 by Dan Krokos

First Edition

10 9 8 7 6 5 4 3 2 1

G475-5664-5-14152

Printed in the United States of America

Library of Congress Cataloging-in-Publication Data
Krokos, Dan.
    False future / Dan Krokos.—First edition.
        pages cm
    Sequel to: False sight.
    Summary: Rhys, Noble, Sophia, and Peter cannot face their enemy,
True Earth, without Miranda; but when they revive her, she is horrified
to find her world in flames and must use her grief to fuel her spirit as
she helps to seek Mr. East, who must be turned in for the brutal enemy
occupation of Manhattan to end.
    ISBN 978-1-4231-4987-3 (hardback)—ISBN 1-4231-4987-4
    [1. Cloning—Fiction.   2. Genetic engineering—Fiction.   3. War—
Fiction.   4. Love—Fiction.   5. Science fiction.]   I. Title.
    PZ7.K9185Faf 2014
    [Fic]—dc23   2014005696

Reinforced binding

Visit www.hyperionteens.com

SUSTAINABLE   Certified Sourcing
FORESTRY
INITIATIVE   www.sfiprogram.org
              SFI-00993

THIS LABEL APPLIES TO TEXT STOCK

to Mom,
for making me read to her in the kitchen

True Earth arrived in Manhattan to finish us off on December 21. They showed up during a whiteout, the worst snowstorm in ten years, which I thought was pretty rude to the citizens of New York. As if trudging through the sloppy streets wasn't hard enough, now they had to deal with an invasion. I had to admire True Earth's brilliance, though. It's hard to organize any kind of resistance when you can't see three feet in front of you. Cruel, but brilliant.

I was sitting at my post in our apartment on the fifty-third floor of 80 Columbus Circle. It was Sophia's turn to be on watch, but she had asked me to cover for her, something about a tension headache. She did that trick where she looked at me and touched my arm and said, "Please, Rhys." Maybe that doesn't qualify as a trick, but it worked. It always works with me.

My post was a chair next to a floor-to-ceiling window overlooking Central Park. Noble told us this is where it would happen, if they came back. And we all knew they would.

The snow was blowing outside the window and sticking in the corners. The endless, swirling white had a hypnotic effect, so every hour I did one hundred push-ups to keep myself sharp. When my eyes couldn't take the white any longer, I started to read a comic book, looking up from the pages every thirty seconds to check on the park. I was in my pajamas, drinking cocoa out of a thick red Christmas mug. At that moment, life wasn't so bad.

At around two in the afternoon, they came. I glanced up from my comic book and peered out the window. Through the white, I saw there was now an enormous black hole in the middle of Central Park. It was a perfect circle—so black, the contrast with the snow hurt my eyes. I knew what it was. I sat there for a moment while the blood drained out of my head. Peace was over. We would have to fight once again. Then I stood up and screamed, *"They're here!"* at the top of my lungs.

Sophia and Noble ran into the room. Peter was at a meeting with some military types about discreetly moving more tanks into the city. While the breadth of True Earth tech wasn't exactly known (Noble wasn't able to provide any specifics on what they might throw at us), the military figured that if they wanted to increase their chances of doing some real damage, it was best to go with shells 120 mm or bigger.

We stood at the window for more time than we should have, but it was impossible to turn away. Flying machines were rising out of the hole like hornets, *dozens* of them, flat and wedge-shaped, wingless. They fired missiles that arced up and over the tops of the skyscrapers, leaving milky trails against the gray winter sky. As we watched, we all knew we should've been preparing for battle, but where do you start? We've fought monsters before, but not an army.

The last few months had been full of preparation: tactics, ground war strategies, training with some of the military's best. But through it all, none of it felt like enough to me. For the last attack True Earth sent thousands of monsters with claws and teeth. Who knew what they would send this time.

Of course, I never dared to say that out loud. Just because my hope was running low didn't mean I wanted to stomp out everyone else's. So I put on a happy face and ran drills with wiry men who had the eyes of killers, all the while knowing I could shred them with my bare hands and that soon people like me would be arriving to fight and kill them.

Now missiles crashed down around the city, creating huge black and orange clouds blurred by the swirling snow. The nearby explosions I could feel through the soles of my feet.

A missile streaked by the window, left to right, and I fell back against the table, ears ringing from the noise, the path of the missile a shadow on my retinas. I knew what True Earth was doing. It was a military tactic the United States was familiar with: shock and awe, also known as rapid dominance. Stun the enemy in the opening moments of battle so they can't organize. Crush their perception of the battlefield and you crush their will to fight. Combine that with the blizzard, and we didn't stand a chance of winning in the opening round. No one said it, but I'm sure we were all thinking the same thing: *We've already lost.*

"We need her," Sophia said. "We need all the help we can get. Or else we should just quit now and leave." More explosions thrummed the glass behind her. She didn't flinch, just stared into my soul with her big brown eyes, which I was perfectly fine with.

But my chest got tight anyway. I missed my friend, but she was at peace. She had done her duty, and it had bought us time. She deserved the break.

Noble didn't say anything at first, which gave me hope. Surely he agreed with me. And not because we were genetically identical, but because it was *right*.

Besides, Peter wasn't here. We couldn't do it without talking to Peter first. And he would say no, I was sure of it.

"We need her," Sophia said again, clearly sensing our hesitation. "There is only the mission now. This is it. This is the time." Sophia's total commitment to our team made it impossible not to love her (even though I hadn't yet worked up the courage to say that to her face). This wasn't her world, but she was willing to fight for it. She was one of us. In the last few months, she'd gone from malnourished girl to a young woman whose dark skin glowed with health. When we jogged in the city, she never lagged behind.

Noble still didn't answer, but I could sense him weighing the options. Finally he said, "We need to find Peter," and walked over to the red phone, the direct line to our military contacts. He picked it up, and I could hear it ringing faintly from the earpiece. Then he held the handset away from his face and looked at it. "It just went dead."

"She would *want* to help," Sophia said, her eyes flitting between Noble and me. "She would."

Noble nodded grimly. "You're right. We have to do it."

"Wait," I said, my throat tightening. We'd always planned to bring her back if we needed the help, and now was certainly that time, but I still hesitated. We had no way of knowing what she would have wanted.

"I don't know," I said.

Noble turned to me with this look on his face that I will remember for the rest of my life. There was pain in the lines around his eyes, the set of his mouth. He had made his decision, but it would haunt him forever.

"Do it, Rhys." At that moment, I think he became my father again. Because though I wasn't sure I wanted to, I was going to do what he said, the way a son is supposed to.

A portion of Central Park was on fire now. There was smoke and snow everywhere, and more things were coming out of the hole. It looked like people, but it was hard to tell from this far away. I didn't want to watch anymore. I'd psyched myself out enough.

I left the window, and Sophia and Noble came with me. The remote was inside a locked case under the sink. Noble pulled a necklace out from under his shirt and tugged once. Hanging from it was the only key to the case, which he pressed into my hand.

I unlocked the case and opened the lid. Inside was a black cube with a single red switch on it, like the kind you'd use to turn on a light. It wasn't labeled. I gripped it with my thumb and forefinger, but stopped there. The switch was such a small, simple thing, yet moving it a half inch would change everything.

Sophia put her slim hand over mine, and in the warmth of her skin I found my strength. I tried to look at her, but it's hard to see through tears.

"We'll do it together," she said.

Then we flipped the switch.

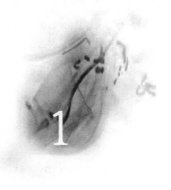

I'm losing blood. The bomb has rolled across the room.

A crippled eyeless swipes my leg from the floor and breaks my shin. It snaps and I go down, fingers tearing at the carpet.

Noah crouches next to me. "C'mon, Miranda. You can do it! You have to do it! Don't give up!"

I pull myself farther along. Noah never leaves my side. "Keep going. Stand up, Miranda. Stand up right now."

The eyeless behind me are a ragged bunch, flopping on the floor in their blood and guts. More are coming up through the hole. My fingers dig at the floor so hard my hands ache. I wiggle up next to the bomb, weak and swimmy, blinking.

I pick up the remote, too dizzy to see straight. Somehow I stand up, all my weight on one leg. I look down and see the hole in my stomach. My blood-slick armor. The pain isn't so bad now. I think that's the blood loss. Can't feel much of anything.

"You can do it," Noah says. He stands next to me, how I remember him. Bright and vibrant and alive. "I believe in you."

He pulls me into a hug and I wrap my arms around him. He isn't really here, but his arms keep me standing all the same. "You can do it," he whispers in my ear. "You're not alone."

The eyeless regroup and surge toward us, circling around like wolves. The nearest one springs, claws outstretched for my throat.

If I push the button, I will save the world.

If I push the button.

I will save the world.

I push the button.

I see the light of fire through my closed eyes and feel pressure too quick to understand. It moves through me, like pain in a dream. I open my eyes and the bright light fades into blue-green. I try to breathe but get a mouthful of something wet and thick. I choke. The floor falls out from under my feet and I slide down, then smack the ground with the back of my head, screaming and coughing on fluid, the pain in my broken leg and torn stomach fading and tingling into nothing, and it

8

doesn't hit me for another second that I'm not dead, that I'm still feeling things, and the fire is gone. I sit up looking for eyeless but of course there are none, and understanding comes in one fell swoop, like a guillotine.

I'm in a small bedroom. A snow-caked window looks out on a redbrick wall.

The empty clone tank behind me is a huge plastic cylinder tilted at a forty-five degree angle. The bottom opened and dumped me and all the weird blue-green fluid onto the floor. There's a TV in the corner coated in a thin layer of dust. The floor is covered in a half inch of fluid.

And I am alone.

"Peter—" I try to call out, but choke instead. I go down on all fours and vomit a long, thin stream of fluid that tastes like nothing. That's when I realize I'm naked. The gel is already cooling on my skin. There's only one reason I would be in a tank. Because I'm not me at all. I'm in a new body, free of burns, holes, broken bones. I died, and yet here I am.

They brought me back.

Why did they bring me back?

Seemingly on its own, my right hand drifts up to the back of my neck. My fingers push through my hair and touch a small, circular piece of metal stuck to the base of my skull. The stamp. There's nothing else it could be, no other way I could be here. There's no other way for me to remember what happened. Somehow they found it, and instead of letting me die for good, they brought me back.

Because they missed me, or because they need me?

I blew myself up to kill the monsters that were planning to literally eat their way through our world. My skin still tingles with the feeling of the explosion. The first microsecond of it anyway, before it turned to brief pain, then nothing at all. Did my death save our world? It better have been for something.

I look at my hands, and they're *my* hands. I'm in a Miranda body. My hair is auburn and shoulder length, like normal. But the scar on my cheek, a horizontal slash courtesy of Mrs. North, is gone. This is my third body. The last time I came back I only remembered scraps of my past. Now I remember everything. I've been dead, but now I'm alive. And I have no idea how to feel about it.

I stand up and don't fall down.

"Noah?" I call out, and get no response. I search for his presence in my head but don't feel him. A shiver rolls through my gut. It sounds like it's thundering outside, but I don't hear rain.

I try again just to be sure. "Noah? Noah, please." But he doesn't respond and I still can't feel him.

He's gone. Truly gone. The stamp must not have saved his identity, his presence within me. All I can feel is the hollow space he left behind.

He deserved more. I say it out loud. "You deserved more."

He might be gone, but I'm not going to stop thinking about him.

I won't let him fade away.

In the corner opposite the TV is a workbench. On top of it is a folded set of black-scaled armor. On top of that is Beacon, my straight sword. The blade is scorched in places, and the hilt is partly melted, but it's intact. There's also a silver revolver leaning against a box of bullets. And a beach towel with little half watermelons on it. The watermelons are dancing. There's nothing else in the room.

Wait, there—a piece of paper half under the towel. I slide it out, and the fluid on my fingers blurs the ink. But it's easy enough to read.

I'm coming to get you. I'm sorry. I love you.
—P

I work my tongue around and spit more fluid. "Peter," I call out again, and it sounds like a sob. It is a sob. They brought me back and I can't do anything but cry. I should be happy. I get to see my team again. I get to look into their eyes, touch them, talk to them. That idea is enough to excite me, if only for the briefest moment.

And Peter is coming to get me. I let that make me feel good

for a few more seconds, until I realize that sound outside isn't thunder. I go to the window and lift it up with both hands. It screeches and jams in the frame, but goes up high enough for me to stick my head out.

Below is a trash-filled alley. Above, the sky is aflame.

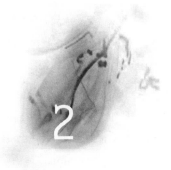

2

The flames disperse into smoke and wreckage that tumbles down from the sky. I hear glass breaking, metal popping, people screaming.

True Earth is here. That's why I'm back. I died to stop their war against us, but clearly it wasn't enough. And my team needs me.

I run to the bench and grab the towel and drag it over my skin. The fluid soaks up easily, leaving my skin feeling fresh and clean and new, which it is. I wrap the towel around my hair to dry it, then unfold my suit of armor with a snap. Putting it on is familiar and calming. I'm not freaking out. I'm not crying. I just know I'm back for a reason, and here are my only possessions in the world.

The armor slides over my damp skin. I push my hands into the attached gloves, wiggle my feet into the socklike bottoms, then shrug into the shoulders. With a little coaxing, the seam in the back seals up to the top of my neck. I feel the suit shifting and contracting, hugging me in places, tightening just a bit around my joints for extra support. When it's over I'm wearing a second skin of black scales.

I grab Beacon off the table. The grip feels different where it melted a little. I swing a practice cut. The balance feels the same, which is all that matters as long as the blade still has its integrity. How embarrassing would it be to get in a sword fight and have my blade snap off? The thought makes me laugh, until I clap my hand over my mouth and tears leak from my eyes.

Don't lose it. You just got back.

And you're needed.

I put Beacon against my spine, and it sticks to the magnetic scales of my armor, the hilt poking above my right shoulder. I open the bedroom door—the frame of which is cracked, most likely from when they brought my tank in—and step into the main room of a musty-smelling apartment. There are two bottles of water on a table in the kitchenette, with a note in Peter's handwriting. *Drink these.* I slam them both. Also on the table is a pair of jeans and a black hooded sweatshirt. A note says—*Wear this, it's cold and your armor is conspicuous. I love you.*

Reading his words has me crying again, but the good kind. Peter loves me. How about that?

I pull the clothes on over my armor. And how thoughtful is this—the sweatshirt even has a hole in the back for Beacon.

A rumble outside rattles the glassware in the cupboards. There are two more things on the table—a syringe filled with a lemonade-colored liquid and yet another note. The note says— *Take this, so you don't forget me.* The shot will keep my memories intact for a while. I ease the needle into my neck, and the blooming heat is familiar, comforting even. Now I'm ready.

I open the apartment door half expecting to see Peter waiting for me. The hallway is jammed with six terrified-looking people talking over one another about the cause of the noise. Two old ladies in nightgowns are holding hands. Everyone freezes when they see me step into the hallway. Maybe it's that they don't recognize me as one of their neighbors. Or maybe it's that I have a sword hilt poking above my shoulder.

"Stay inside," I tell them. "Fill up as many containers as you can with water."

They stay frozen, even though I just gave them really good advice. Another explosion shakes dust from the ceiling.

"Move!" I charge down the hallway to the stairwell, burst through the door, and jump from landing to landing. I'm through the front door five seconds later.

Bitter-cold air hits me in the face, bringing with it the smell of smoke. Snowflakes melt on my cheeks. The explosions are ten times as loud now, rattling my eardrums, and I can see columns of smoke rising all around the city. People are running in all directions, and strange jets zoom between the buildings above us, heating the air as they pass. I don't understand; it wasn't supposed to be like this. True Earth wanted to preserve our world for resettlement, but now they're here with bombs. It's like they've decided that blowing us all to hell is the easy way. A missile hits a building to my left, blowing a cloud of glass onto the people in the street.

The eyeless are something I can fight. But how do we stop this?

I jog down the sidewalk with no real plan—I don't know how to find my team unless they find me first. There are people everywhere, slipping and sliding in the snow. Clearly they don't have a plan; they're just running. Running home maybe, though they must know they won't be safe there, either. The chaos is everywhere. The street is clogged with wrecked cars all jammed together. People are standing on their hoods, looking up at the smoky sky with wide eyes. The scene reminds me of last summer, when a handful of Roses brought Cleveland to its knees. I just stand there for a moment, stunned. I died for nothing. Nothing at all. Maybe I even drove them to this by destroying the eyeless.

A honking horn pulls my attention to the right. Coming

toward me on the sidewalk is a blacked-out Taurus with a light bar on top and antennae sticking up from the trunk—a government car. It slows to a stop on the sidewalk and people rush past it on both sides. A man's hip knocks off the passenger mirror.

Rhys is behind the wheel. His blond hair is hidden inside a hooded sweatshirt, but his face is clear. We stare at each other for a beat. I'm so happy to see him, but terrified at the same time. Peter said he was coming to get me, so why is Rhys here? Rhys gets out of the car and we rush each other. He hugs me and lifts me up and spins us around. When he puts me down there are tears in his eyes.

"You're back," he says.

"Just in time for the party." I mean to say it lightly, but it comes out dark. "Peter?"

Rhys gives a short laugh. "What, I'm not good enough?" He smiles. "Pete's busy. You'll see him soon." He shakes his head and the smile falls. "I'm so sorry."

"Save it for later. We have work to do." I head for the driver's door—I want to drive, not sit—but someone slips behind the wheel first. Some random guy in a red flannel jacket and chunky black glasses. He looks up at me and tries to pull the door shut, but I hold it fast. It doesn't even budge. He yanks on it twice more, saying, "Let go! Jesus, girl, *let go.*"

"You really picked the wrong car."

He holds eye contact with me for about one second, then decides I'm right.

I can tell Rhys thought a lot about what to say next. He starts with, "So . . ." followed by, "how are you holding up?"

"Fine."

"You know, I've been thinking about you coming back."

"Oh yeah?"

"Yeah. And I don't want you to feel like you're not real again. Like you're less of a person."

I don't feel like less of a person, exactly. I don't know what I feel. I do know that you can't be dead for weeks, or months, and then come back in a new body and be the same. You just can't.

"Okay."

"I mean, all people are basically clones of themselves. As we grow, our cells are constantly replaced by new cells. Eventually there isn't an atom inside of us that was there at the start. But we're still ourselves. You know? I think that's really cool."

The snowy road blurs until I blink away the tears. I put my hand on Rhys's knee. "Thank you," I say. It's a nice idea, and I appreciate him saying it, but it's not quite the same. I died. And now I'm back. Inside, I can still see the eyeless. How they encircled me, came at me with their claws and teeth. How it feels like just minutes ago they tore holes in my flesh.

I thought I was doing some great thing by sacrificing myself, but it doesn't feel that way now. It feels pointless.

The plan was to stop an invasion of our planet. A parallel universe had released monsters that were meant to systematically kill us one by one, leaving our world intact. I led the monsters into a different world, gathered them up, and exploded them. And myself. Yet the other universe is back. I didn't stop them at all.

Rhys smiles. "No problem."

A loud roar from the front—I look forward in time to see a tank coming right for us. I assess the threat—it's an M1 Abrams. Our guys.

"Please maneuver," Rhys says calmly, and I swing the car up onto the sidewalk, knocking over a mailbox that trips two running people. That's when I see it's not just one tank but a whole line of them. Five in all, roaring right up Broadway. They crunch past any cars in the way, pushing them aside like they're nothing, even running over a few, smashing them down into the snow. Glass explodes from the windows—*pop pop pop!*

"Keep going!" Rhys says.

"That isn't going to be enough, Rhys," I say, panic creeping into my voice. "A few tanks? Against True Earth?"

"There's more—tanks and troops all over the city. But even so . . . I don't know if it's enough. They opened a hole in Central Park, and it's big."

"Is the military organizing?"

I swing back onto the road, my right wheels down in a rut created by the tank treads.

"I don't know," Rhys says. "Noble tried to make contact, but the phone is dead. I'm sure they're not sitting on their asses at this point. We'll try to rendezvous with the military after meeting up with Noble and Sophia."

"How are they? Noble, Sophia?"

"Great. Noble has been swamped with preparations, and I think he'd be dead without Sophia."

As we zip down Broadway I see people coming out of stores, their arms full of stuff. Looters. As I watch, two men carry a sofa through the front door of a furniture store. The attack has just started, and people have already succumbed to their baser desires. For the briefest second, I see True Earth's point of view. We really can be animals.

A spinning chunk of building falls from the sky and crashes in the intersection just ahead of us. "Whoa!" Rhys screams as it bounces once and begins to roll toward us. I grab the door handle and prepare to dive out, but Rhys reaches across and jerks the wheel sideways, saying, "Hold on!" We keep sliding toward the tumbling chunk, but the front tires catch in time, and the debris smashes into the rear fender. The impact spins us sideways into a light pole. My head smacks against the side

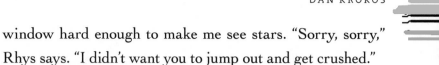
window hard enough to make me see stars. "Sorry, sorry," Rhys says. "I didn't want you to jump out and get crushed."

I hit the gas, but there's a terrible grinding sound from the front, and we don't go anywhere.

Just ahead there's a subway stop with the numbers 1 2 3 centered in red circles.

"The subway," I say, pointing.

Rhys is already getting out of the car. We jog over to the stairs. "Good idea. There's a stop right outside our building. Even if the trains aren't running we can move through the tunnels and avoid the mob."

Right before we reach the station a car zooms through the intersection, heading west from Central Park. It's unlike any car I've ever seen. An armored Corvette is the closest description, with huge knobby tires in the front and back. It emits a high-pitched whine.

"What the hell is that?" Rhys says as we watch it go. It slams nose-first into a taxi but doesn't slow down; the ramp-like front end just flips the taxi out of the way. It swings around a corner and is gone.

"C'mon," I say, jogging down the steps into the subway.

We hop the turnstile and jog onto the platform, which somehow feels colder than outside. It's crowded with people. Five cops try to maintain order, telling people to stay calm, to stay put, that a train will be along shortly. The little booth that sells candy and pop is shuttered, but that doesn't keep two men from working on the lock with a couple screwdrivers. The cops don't seem to notice or care.

"Should we just jog the tunnel?" I ask. Better to move independently than get stuck in a metal tube with terrified citizens.

"Let's wait a minute," Rhys says, eyeing the cops and the anxious crowd. "They might need our help."

Just then I feel a push of air coming down the tunnel and hear a high whistle that grows louder by the second. A train is coming. People immediately crowd on the yellow line, jostling to be first. A young girl almost falls onto the tracks, but her father snatches her puffy jacket in time.

One of the cops steps forward, waving his baton and flashlight. "Everybody get back! Stand *BACK*!"

The train is still thirty seconds away, so I ask Rhys, "What'd I miss while I was out?"

"A lot. Noble talked to the president after you . . . did your thing."

"Blew myself up."

He touches my arm, then lets his hand fall away, averting his eyes. I guess talking about my death so bluntly makes him uncomfortable. "Yes. The government put us up in New York, since Noble said they'd strike here first. Looks like the old man was right."

The train is still coming. I can see the headlights now, far back in the tunnel.

"Noble found your memory disk thing in the wreckage of the Verge, but Peter argued against bringing you back. He said it wasn't right, since we could never know what *you* wanted. But they came to an agreement—you would only be brought back if True Earth returned."

"Because you'd need all the help you can get."

"Right. We went to Cleveland and took one of the blank—ah, I mean you, from Key Tower, and drove you to the other apartment. We wanted you to be in a separate location in case they found us and attacked there first. Noble set us up with these internal heart monitors and connected them to your tank. So if one of us died, you would've been activated automatically."

I think about the row of blank Mirandas, all waiting to become someone. I could've been any one of them. I wonder how they picked this body.

I imagine being in their position, trying to figure out if they should bring someone back from the dead. What would I do? What's a fair reason to bring someone back? What if I just *missed* the person?

Maybe I'm glad Noah doesn't have to deal with any of this ever again.

"What did you think? About bringing me back."

Rhys doesn't answer. I decide to let it go.

The train swishes past us, not slowing down. It keeps going, right through the station. The weirdest thing is, I can't see anybody through the windows as it goes past us.

The crowd starts shouting. A cop blows his whistle again and again.

Once it's halfway into the tunnel, I hear the train's power shut off and the wheels scrape along the track. The whole thing comes to a stop about two hundred feet past the platform. The taillights glow like demon eyes in the darkness before they wink out. People on the platform start yelling again.

Rhys and I share a look. Then we jump down onto the tracks and start jogging, careful to avoid the electrified third rail. We both stop once we're in the darkness of the tunnel. A dozen brave/stupid people are following us.

"If another train comes, they'll be crushed," I say, "if they aren't electrocuted."

Rhys nods. "We need to keep them away. You got this one? I'm due for a shot. . . ."

"Yeah, I got it." I release a small wave of fear, just enough to discourage anyone from following us into the tunnel. The always-there pressure in my brain swells at first, then lessens, bringing a sweet-and-sour feeling that makes my scalp tingle. The center of my brain feels hot, almost pleasantly so, like a heated stone wrapped in a blanket.

The people following us turn around; two trip on the tracks but scramble to their feet. "What is it? What is it?" one of them says as they nearly launch themselves back onto the platform. None of them will have an answer.

"Nicely done," Rhys says.

We turn our attention back to the train.

The emergency lights are on inside the rear car, but I don't see anybody. I hop up onto the back and pull the door open, stepping into the dim yellow light.

The car is empty, but the seats and floor are covered in blood.

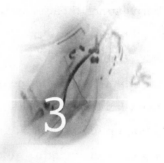

3

W e pull our swords in unison. Rhys grabs a Glock from under his sweatshirt. We hold still, listening. The door snicks shut behind us, and now it's completely silent, except for the soft thumps of explosions up above.

"What do you think?" Rhys whispers.

This isn't the style of a Rose. This is the style of a monster. "I thought I destroyed all the eyeless."

We move through the car, stepping over and around smears of blood. The smears all go in the same direction, telling us the eyeless boarded from the rear, slashing with their claws and biting with their teeth. Wounding people, driving them forward to the front of the car. I see the first few bodies just inside the next car—an old woman on her back, a man in a blue suit on his side, and a guy who got stuck between the cars.

The door keeps trying to shut on his ankle. It opens and closes, opens and closes.

I turn my head and close my eyes, swallowing hard. Then I trip on a grocery bag, spilling eggs onto the floor. Three of them break, and the yolks mix with blood.

"You okay?" Rhys asks, eyes forward like mine should be.

"Yes." I have to be. We keep moving. Someone's tablet is still playing a TV show, the screen fractured.

We step over the guy in the door. I nudge his ankle aside, and the door closes behind us.

I follow Rhys as fast as my gelatin legs will allow. We get through two more cars, where more people have bunched together and died in clumps. My neck stiffens with each passing second, as if someone is driving a screw into the top of my spine. It's so quiet I can hear us breathing.

The fifth car is in complete darkness, save one flickering emergency light right above a slumped-over form. In the darkness to my left, something drips on the floor.

Rhys presses a button on his Glock, and a little flashlight snaps on. Handy. The light is sterile and white. He swings it left and right, and we creep forward. At the end of the car is a rhythmic banging, like a drum. Another door sliding open and closed, open and closed.

"You scared?" Rhys says.

My pulse tells me yes. I'd rather be back in the tank. But I'm glad to have Rhys by my side. "I'm fine."

We make it to the front of the train, where we find even more bodies. Most of these are young people who were able to outrun the others. The door at the front of the train yawns wide open, nothing but darkness and silence beyond. I creep toward it and slowly pull the door shut.

Rhys uses his Glock to smash open the operator's booth in the front right corner of the car. The little booth is empty; I have no idea where the operator went, or why the train lost power. Maybe trains are down across the city. Through the windshield the darkness is unchanged.

"Where are the lights?" Rhys says.

The controls are half digital, half analog. I find a little box on the screen that says FRONT LIGHTS. I jab it with my finger, and the tunnel lights up bright yellow. As my eyes adjust, shapes come into view. They are monsters.

But they are not the eyeless.

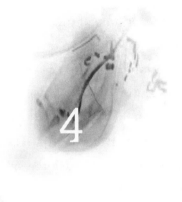

4

The creatures are twitching, shifting back and forth. They don't have bodies. They just have arms—*human* arms—eight black limbs connected together in a ball of muscle. Each arm ends with a hand, five fingers tipped in claws. They're like massive spiders without the bodies. My throat closes, and Rhys makes a strangled sound, muttering "Oh my God" under his breath. On the tracks I see a body clad in a blue uniform—the train operator.

I swallow. It feels like swallowing a rock. The black hands lift up and open toward us, like they're seeing with their palms.

My heart is pounding so hard I can feel it against the inside of my ribs. Rhys actually grabs my wrist and squeezes, like a reflex. I try to beat down my fear with anger—*These FREAKS killed all those people. What are you going to do about it?*

The spiders are crammed together, their black arms slick with blood. Their claws click on the tracks, and a few hunker down low before jumping onto the front of the train. *Thump thump thump.* They're coming back for us.

"Go!" Rhys screams.

I find a lever on the dashboard. The only lever. I jam it forward with glee, ready to crush the spiders under tons and tons of metal.

But nothing happens.

"Where's the ON button?" Rhys says.

A spider now plastered to the front of the car starts slamming one clawed hand into the windshield. Its hand is the size of a large frying pan. The glass splinters on the second swing. Rhys lines his Glock up and fires a bullet through the window into the twisted mass of muscle and tendons where the spider's arms meet. It drops out of sight.

In the meantime, the rest have jumped onto the car and are shaking it back and forth like monkeys.

One of them grabs the door handle at the front.

"No!" I snatch the handle as it dips down, heaving up with all my strength, but then it tears the handle out of my hands. The spider flings open the door, which rebounds viciously, and the creature recoils, then slams it open again. This time the door pops out of its hinges at the top.

"Rhys!"

Rhys fires a blind shot, then stabs at the spider with his sword. He slams the door again and pushes a little locking pin through it. Still, it's halfway out of the frame, and two fingers curl around the top, jerking on the door.

"Get us moving, Miranda." Glass shatters at the other end of the car.

I search the dash while another spider hops up on the windshield. There's a key, which I turn so hard I'm surprised I don't break it. The train comes to life with a loud hum and rattle. I jab the lever forward and we accelerate.

"Faster!" Rhys calls out.

"I'm trying!"

Some spiders are trying to pry apart the double doors on the side of the car; there's just enough space for them to fit between the train and the wall of the tunnel. As I watch, two spiders still hanging on to the front of the train get knocked off by a stoplight, limbs flailing, hands opening and closing. I almost shout *YES* at the top of my lungs.

With the lever pushed all the way forward, the train picks up so much speed I have to brace myself against the door. Another spider jumps onto the front of the train and wiggles its claw through the hole in the window left by Rhys's bullet. It thrashes, widening the hole, bits of glass jabbing into flesh. It doesn't seem to feel pain. I shove my sword through the hole as we barrel into the next station. The lighted platform is crowded with people and we fly by them, back into the tunnel. *Sorry, you're going to want the next train.*

I lock the accelerator in place, then join Rhys in the middle of the car. We stand back-to-back. A spider crawls along the ceiling; another crouches on a nearby bench. Suddenly they turn away and move toward the other end of the car. The ones working on the side door are gone. *Why?*

I turn around as we burst into the next station—there's a train stopped ahead. I slip back into the booth and yank the lever all the way toward me. The wheels kick up two trails of sparks, and I smack my head against the half-broken windshield. We're a hundred feet from the train, then fifty, not slowing fast enough.

"We need to jump!" Rhys says, and I'm already prying open the side doors, finishing the work the spiders started. I push one halfway open, people rushing past the opening just feet away.

"You first!" I scream, shoving Rhys at the door. He jumps through, tucking himself into a roll. I do the same as the two trains collide hard enough to feel through the air. Like the first two, the platform is crowded with dozens of startled people.

"Up up up!" Rhys shouts at them. *"Up the stairs!"*

Maybe it's our swords, or the spider blood on us, but the people do as they're told. We follow them up a few flights, watching for spiders behind us, and emerge in Columbus Circle, right at the southwest corner of Central Park.

Aboveground it's chaos, like before. More of those strange armored cars are zooming around, crashing into the regular cars and shoving them aside like toys. People are fleeing out of the park, kicking up snow with their boots. Through the leafless trees I can see a dozen fires glowing and bodies and vehicles moving with purpose, the steady onward march of an invasion. It's not the temperature that makes me cold.

A taxi is idling on the sidewalk next to me, all four doors open. Someone tries to get behind the wheel, but I dart past them, slip into the driver's seat, ram it into gear, then floor it up and over the curb, wheels breaking loose on the snow.

"Miranda!" Rhys calls after me. But I'm not going far. I swing the car around and drive it straight down the subway stairs. The walls slam all four doors shut. The wheels bounce down the steps as a spider is rounding the bend, ready to come up and claw whatever it can. The front of the taxi hits it, and the whole car jams on the first landing of the stairwell at a sideways angle, pinning the spider and leaving no room for any others to squeeze through. Two of the pinned spider's arms poke up from behind the bumper and slam down, gouging

33

wide gashes in the hood of the taxi. They scrape and dig and twitch and then stop.

Rhys is already on the trunk of the cab, breaking the back window with his boot. It comes out in one fractured piece, and he grabs my hand and pulls me out. The spiders scream (*how?*) down in the station before moving away, looking for another exit. They'll find one soon, but maybe I've bought some time.

We climb the stairs and head toward the twin skyscrapers of the Time Warner Center. Idiots are running out the front door with expensive-looking clothes and—I swear to God—copper pots and pans.

Suddenly a voice booms out, only it's inside my head somehow, like telepathy. I know everyone around me can hear it too, because they all *stop dead*. Frozen in time.

"Greetings, people of New York. I am the leader of the army currently invading your city. Do not fear. We mean you only as much harm as necessary."

I know the voice—it belongs to the director of True Earth. The Original Miranda North I'm cloned from.

"There is something on the island of Manhattan that we desire. When we find it, we will depart, and you will never see us again. Meanwhile, do not try to leave. As I speak, powerful turrets are being placed around the perimeter of the island. Nothing will get in or out, I assure you. Your country will try to fly planes and satellites over our

airspace, and they will be shot down. But I repeat—we mean you only as much harm as necessary. Follow instructions and you will be safe. Those found acting out of order will be destroyed."

Two gunshots echo off the buildings, the source impossible to discover.

"Flyers will be distributed. They will show you what we seek. The sooner we find what we want, the sooner your city will be returned to you. Take heart, citizens of New York. This is not your end."

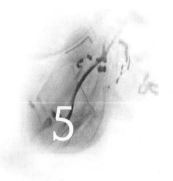

5

The silence that follows seems to leave people dazed. A woman drops the new computer monitor she was carrying. Some people just stand around, looking up at the sky, waiting for more. Then a cab driver honks at someone standing in the street, breaking the spell. Soon many are running again, but they're not as panicked now, as if the promise they aren't *all* going to die is comforting.

Someone actually screams, "IS THIS A JOKE?"

A man in a blue pinstriped suit is yelling into a phone until someone plucks it from his ear and darts toward the subway escalator.

"Don't!" I shout, but he's already gone.

"We have our work cut out for us," Rhys whispers.

Through the trees I see more people moving toward us, but at a steady march. Definitely not pedestrians.

I take Rhys's hand. "We need to get inside."

He leads me to the north side of the nearest tower, to a posh entrance. The doorman booth is unmanned. We get into one of the elevators, and Rhys uses a key, then jabs the button labeled 53. While it rises, I count my falling pulse. I can still hear the director's words in my head, clearer than memory. I don't buy that they're not here to harm us, especially since they've already fired missiles around the city, but I do believe they're looking for something. Our first order of business should be to nab one of those flyers.

The elevator door opens onto a spacious foyer. Floor-to-ceiling windows are straight ahead, looking over the park. I run to them. Half of Central Park is on fire, but even as I watch, odd-looking aircraft hovering over the blaze spray foam that extinguishes the fire at once. It's hard to make out details from this far away, but the jets are clearly not from this world. They're rectangular, with one vertical engine in each of the four corners. In the streets more of those strange cars are racing around.

From the south, four American fighter jets fly in low over the tops of buildings, their heavy guns firing, bright yellow tracers against the gray sky. Seeing them makes my chest swell with hope. So much for the director's promise that none would get through. One of True Earth's jets explodes in a red and black fireball. *Yes!* The other True Earth planes break formation, taking off at high velocities in random directions, like UFOs. The American jets are gone, circling around the northern tip of Manhattan for another pass.

Closer, toward the middle of Central Park, I can see the edges of the Black. It's a familiar void in the shape of a circle, a hole in the very fabric of our world. I never wanted to see it again, and I thought I would never have to.

On foot, the Rose army pours out of the park and advances south. Groups of them filter through the streets in that same steady march I saw outside.

"Miranda," a familiar voice says behind me.

When I turn, Noble stands there just as I remember him: tall, blond, and bearded, with a smile that you can't help but let warm you. I only saw him a day ago, but to him it's been months.

"Peter's not back yet?" I knew as soon as I entered the apartment. Somehow I could feel it.

"No, he isn't."

There's a kindness in his eyes that I last saw from Dr. Tycast. Noble holds his arms out and I hug him, briefly.

"I'm sorry," is all he says, and I accept.

"I understand."

I finally take a look around the apartment. To my right

is an open kitchen stacked with boxes of gear. The breakfast table is littered with guns and ammunition. I see a grapnel gun with a spool of wire, like the one Tobias used to keep me and Grace from falling to our deaths last summer.

"Noble got us some new toys," Rhys says. "He's been scrounging while you were gone, borrowing from the military when they let him."

"These aren't toys," I say, running a finger over the barrel of an assault rifle.

"You know what I mean," he replies. And I do. "You should see the guest bedroom. He turned it into a lab for making memory shots out of stuff you can buy in a bodega."

I smile my thanks at Noble. Rhys and Peter are capable of taking care of themselves, no doubt. Still, knowing Noble was watching over them, I feel better about my absence.

Sophia walks in from another room and gives me a hug. Her black hair has grown out enough to tie into a short pony-tail. She must've put on ten pounds of muscle. No doubt she's been training with Rhys and Noble. Now that she's not eating out of a gutter, she doesn't look like a frail little girl anymore.

"It's so good to see you," she says, like we're old friends who just haven't had a chance to hang out in a while.

I nod. "You too."

To no one in particular, I say, "I need to go to the roof."

"This way," Noble says.

We take the elevator up.

"Peter was meeting with troops the government has hidden in the city when the attack began," Noble says on the ride. "I haven't been able to reach him on the comm. It seems all communications are down."

"I was worried about Rhys out there all alone," Sophia says to me. "I'm glad he had you to protect him."

Rhys snorts, then sobers quickly. Sophia gives him a playful shove. He catches her hand and holds it for a second, before letting it drop reluctantly. *Interesting.*

"So if Peter was working with the government," I say, continuing where Noble left off, "where's the counterstrike? I saw some jets and tanks, but that's it. Where's the defense?"

"We're not going to win with force alone," Noble says. "Throwing everything we have into one assault will only result in us losing. We need an edge. We need to organize, *then* strike."

"While people die," I say.

No one responds.

The doors open at the roof, revealing the Hudson River and New Jersey beyond it. Everything is cold and gray from this height, though the snow has abated to flurries.

The wind catches my hood and flips it down. We walk to the edge of the roof and see exactly what True Earth meant when they said the perimeter has been secured. Several of those four-engine jets hover near the waterline, dropping box-shaped loads. As we watch, the boxes unfold and enormous guns that take up two lanes of the highway are left standing. There seems to be a gun every hundred feet. As soon as the first jets bank away into the city, more swoop in and continue to drop boxes.

Across the river, two military helicopters hover near the shore of New Jersey. The guns down on the highway swivel on their bases until they're lined up with the helos, then contract suddenly, crackling with blue electricity. Across the river the two helicopters explode in enormous clouds of flame.

"My God," Noble says.

Farther off, more military jets cut back and forth across the sky, but don't dare come any closer.

"Look at this!" Rhys yells. He's at the other end of the roof. We jog over, my heart already in my throat. The view of the park is even more breathtaking from up here. The column of smoke must be a mile across. It curls away toward the east, over Queens. Nearer the ground, twenty of the strange four-engine jets are supporting what appears to be a thick metal disk several hundred feet across. The disk hangs in between them, suspended by cables. We watch as they lower the disk into the middle of the park. It completely covers the Black, which seems impossible because that's where the disk had to have come through.

As soon as the disk is in place the jets flash with small bursts of light, and I realize they've shot at something, but I can't see what. Almost immediately there are several explosions in the trees, followed by the sound of cracking wood and the swish/scrape of branches as dozens of trees fall. I see glimpses of the wreckage as wind clears the smoke. They were tanks. The tanks we passed on Broadway.

Now I realize it doesn't matter what else the military has planned. We're on our own.

"What's the disk?" Rhys asks.

Before anyone can answer, movement on the roof of our building's south tower catches my eye. Two people are watching us from behind the railing, their postures rigid. They're wearing armor like ours, but in dark red, not black. It's too far away to make out details, but I recognize the auburn hair—my auburn hair—of a Miranda, and the blond locks of a Rhys clone. A moment passes where we just look at one another, completely confused, before they push off the railing together and sprint for the stairs.

On the north tower, Rhys and I do the same, a half second behind. We don't even talk about it.

"Use the grapnel guns!" Noble shouts after us. "There are two!" He knows the stakes—the Roses are fleeing because they're going to report our location, if they haven't already. *How did they know it was us?* But then I have the answer. Had it just been me and Rhys, we might've been able to play it off, but not with Noble and Sophia there too.

We take the elevator to the apartment. Rhys grabs the grapnel guns from the breakfast table while I make myself busy throwing a chair through the middle window. Or trying to. The chair bounces off the glass, but I pick it up again and ram it through the window, shaking it around to break up the safety glass while cold air pumps into the room. So much for having a safe house. But it's not like we have a choice.

The mix of warm and cold air makes my nose run. Rhys tosses me a grapnel gun. My eyes scan the room, looking for the best anchor point. We've been inside for fifteen seconds. If their elevator was already at the top, they could be halfway down by now.

"How does this work?" I say as I realize it just has a trigger and a switch marked SHOOT/RETRACT.

Rhys shoots his at the floor, and the pointed end buries itself in the concrete under the carpet. I do the same. The recoil is so powerful it almost flies out of my hand.

"Like this," he says, pinching the cable with both feet. "Squeeze the trigger to slow. But hurry."

He holds the gun with both hands and dives backward out the window.

"Oh," I say.

Rhys flies toward the ground, the gun buzzing in his hands

as it rapidly unspools. I jump after him headfirst, realizing how insane this is. Have I even been back for an hour yet?

I tuck my chin to my chest and keep my hands firm on the handle; the cord scrapes between my feet as it unspools, a high scream. Below me the pavement grows closer by the second, as the wind freezes the tears in my eyes and whips my hair against my face. I squeeze the trigger and my descent slows; the blood rushes into my head, making it feel like it's about to burst. *Don't let go.* Rhys is way ahead of me, almost all the way to the bottom. I keep steady pressure on the trigger as the sounds of the city get louder. People are still jogging on the sidewalks, and traffic is bumper-to-bumper, too many cars abandoned for there to be a proper flow again. Ten feet from the bottom, I let go of the gun and backflip onto my feet, instantly dizzy as the blood rushes out of my head. Rhys steadies me with his hand, and two seconds later we're sprinting around the front of the building.

"Where will they come out?" I ask breathlessly.

"Probably the south side!"

We skid around the corner onto 58th Street, then pull up short next to another American tank. This one looks abandoned, the hatch on top wide open, its engine idling raucously. But that's not what has my attention. Straight ahead is one of True Earth's strange armored vehicles, parked against the curb as if the driver just needed to run into the drugstore or something. It must belong to the other Miranda and Rhys. We made it in time.

I pull Beacon off my back as we approach the exit, and sure enough, twenty seconds later the two Roses in red burst out, heading right for the tank-car. If they make it there first, it's over, we can't stop them. We close the distance as fast as we can while staying semi-silent, our footsteps muffled by the snow on the street. I make it to the Miranda first. She turns at my approach, and I grab her arm as it reaches forward to block me. I spin her around, palming the back of her neck, and then slam her forehead into the side door, knocking her unconscious.

Rhys wrestles with his clone behind me.

"A little help . . ." he puffs.

I grab the clone's leg as he kicks at my knee, then kick him right back in a place that is not his knee. He howls and goes slack, and Rhys sweeps the clone's other leg hard enough to spin him in midair, so he cracks his head on the street and lies still.

I kneel next to the Miranda, fingers going to her neck, eyes on the space around us. "Is he dead?"

Rhys checks for a pulse on his clone. "No, not yet."

People on the street have stopped to watch us, including a fireman wearing full gear.

"Move along!" I scream at them.

The fireman starts to say something, but then one of True Earth's jets slews around the corner high above, and the downdraft knocks him over. The jet slows to a hover and heat washes down from the engines, the noise a compression on my skin. I stagger under the blast, the snow around me turning to steam. People scatter like roaches, and I'm about to take cover when pieces of paper begin to float down to the street, shooting out from the bottom of the jet. They fill the air, blown around by the wind.

I snatch one.

The top says FIND THIS MAN.

The bottom says REPORT/DELIVER HIM TO THE NEAREST INVADER.

Well, at least they're honest about who they are.

In the middle is a picture of a man I recognize, though I've never seen him before. He looks like my ex-boyfriend, Noah, who erased my memories, then died trying to protect me. Only this man is about thirty years older.

It's Noah East—*Mr. East*—one of our creators.

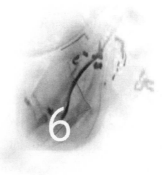

6

"Rhys..." I begin.

"It can wait," he barks. He heaves his clone onto the rear of the tank-car. "Grab the other one."

I shove the paper into my jeans pocket, then pick up the dead weight of my own clone. There's a little badge on her armor, just under the hollow of her throat. It reads M-96. I take her weapons—a sword like mine and an assault rifle that's too futuristic-looking for this world—and then lift her onto the vehicle next to the Rhys clone.

Rhys touches the door, and it slides upward with a metallic hiss. Inside it looks like a space shuttle. "I'm going to park this thing in the garage, then take our new friends up to the apartment. Go around front and make sure no reinforcements are coming."

He shuts the door without waiting for a response. The tank starts up with a low whine that steadily rises as he drives away. The two limp clones on the back bounce with the bumps but don't roll off. The sight makes me laugh for some reason.

I head around the front, face hidden within my hood, hands in my pockets, as inconspicuous as I can be. Though maybe I'd blend in better if I were walking around dazed. People still seem confused after that mental announcement from the director.

From the front of the building, I watch as the Rose army keeps coming from the park. Most of them are in black scales, but some wear silver, red, or white. I watch them for a beat; none are moving toward me. So far so good.

The nearest pack comes across a group of people, who try to flee, but the Roses hold up their hands like, *It's okay, we're not going to hurt you!* And the people stop. How are they controlling them? I open my sixth sense but feel no fear waves coming off the intruders.

The Roses surround them and shine laser pointers in their eyes, one after another. I assume it's a scanner of some kind. *They're searching for East.* If he's as smart as us, he'd be wearing a disguise, and the Roses know it.

After a minute, the Roses continue on, leaving the people even more confused.

I give it another two minutes, then decide it's safe and head inside.

Rhys already has the Roses tied to metal chairs when I get there. The Rhys clone has a badge on his uniform like the Miranda; his reads R-34. Both clones are still knocked out, chins on their chests. M-96 has a wicked purple-and-red bruise on her forehead. Behind them, Sophia is busy taping cardboard over the broken window, but the wind is barreling in, flapping the cardboard viciously.

"Good work," Noble says as I walk inside. He guides me to the kitchen, and I let him. There is a protein shake and a ham sandwich on the counter, plus two more bottles of water. Next to the food is a huge map of Manhattan, certain neighborhoods circled with red ink. His too-small handwriting is scrawled all over the map.

"Thank you," I say as Noble leans over the map, pen in hand. My nose is still numb from the cold. I down a bottle of water and eat half the sandwich, then approach the two Roses.

"We should let them wake up on—" Rhys begins, but my slap across M-96's face interrupts him. "Or we could do that."

I give R-34 a hard slap next.

M-96 wakes up first, blinking her eyes at different times like some weird doll coming to life. She swivels her head around, taking in her surroundings. "Let us go," she says.

"Sure," I say.

She stares at me.

"What are you doing here?" I say.

R-34 wakes with a gasp. He jerks in his bindings. Behind them, Noble has traded the pen for a shotgun. He always has our backs.

"What are you doing here?" I say again.

"Have you seen the flyer?" M-96 says. She might as well spit the words; I know how angry she feels.

"Flyer?" Noble asks.

I pull the paper from my pocket and pass it to him. Noble's eyebrows go up when he recognizes East, and he says, "Hmm. I've aged better."

"So you lock down the island to find one man?" Rhys says.

R-34 is glaring at Rhys. "You're a traitor," he says. "You were raised to study this world, not defend it."

"And who are you?" M-96 spits at me. "You're not the Miranda from Alpha. She's dead. Blew herself up."

"Unless you came back to life?" R-34 says, smirking.

I don't answer.

"Interesting," he continues, my silence all the confirmation he needs. "How much do you remember this time?"

How do they know so much about us?

Without a word, Rhys kicks R-34 in the chest. The chair tips backward and slams down. R-34 loses his breath and twists back and forth. But now he can see Sophia putting the last few pieces of tape on the window.

He laughs a kind of victory laugh as we pull him upright. The next second, as my hand is closing around his throat, I pick up the scent of roses.

"No!" I punch him in the face, but M-96 is releasing waves of her own, adding her power to his. Noble takes a step back, his face contorted with fear, though he's conditioned himself against the energy, like the other creators.

But Sophia hasn't. She shrieks, making my ears ring. She's already sobbing, backpedaling, her hands going to her face, fingers curling into claws. We all scream her name—"SOPHIA!" She takes one step, two, then three. Her shoulders hit the cardboard, which bows outward. The tape groans on the window, stretching, stretching as she writhes, but she can't twist away from the waves of terror.

Rhys lunges for her and grabs her wrist as she bursts through the cardboard. "I GOT YOU!"

I shove R-34 onto his back so hard he bounces, then leap

over him to help Rhys. Sophia almost pulls Rhys through the window after her, but he claps his palm on the glass with enough grip to hold them both. Sophia is clawing at his arm, trying to slip out of his grasp, thrashing back and forth.

"Sophia, stop!" Rhys says, leaning farther out the window.

Noble and I are there in the next second. I grab Sophia's other arm, the cold air a slap in the face, and Noble grabs Rhys from behind, anchoring him until we can pull them both back inside. Sophia keeps trying to slip free, her arms a blur, fingers scratching at our faces, until Rhys pins her arms to her sides, holding her from behind, lifting her off the ground.

I march over to R-34 and kick him in the temple hard enough to make him stop. His waves fade away, the scent of roses replaced with the scent of smoke-tinged air from outside. His eyelids flutter before going still. Sophia is still thrashing and crying.

"Stop the other one, Miranda!" Rhys shouts, craning his face away so Sophia doesn't break his nose with the back of her head.

I straddle M-96 and choke her until the scent of roses disappears completely. Her eyes bulge and little capillaries in her cheeks and eyes burst.

"Miranda, that's enough," Noble says. *"Enough."*

I go a second longer, then release her. I drag her into the bathroom, which is enormous and mostly marble, then slam the door. Sophia is sobbing in the other room—breathless, choking sobs, her anguish like needles in my ears. I shove M-96 in the chest, and she falls backward until the chair hits the bathtub, leaving her tilted at a forty-five degree angle.

M-96 is breathing heavily now, staring at me with wide eyes. I guess that's what I look like when I'm afraid.

I take Beacon off my back and settle the point in the hollow of her throat, right above her little badge.

"I've just been resurrected for the second time, and my feelings about that are a little complicated. Especially when I died thinking it would make a difference."

Her eyes go even wider than before. "You *are* her."

"Yup. And I don't have any patience. None. Tell me what the director wants so badly from East and I won't shove this through your throat. If you don't . . . well, at least your neck is hovering over a bathtub."

She closes her eyes and swallows once.

I'm almost surprised when she opens her mouth and starts talking. Almost.

"East possesses an item of great importance." Her words come out in a rush, like she's trying to finish before she has second thoughts.

I set the sword on the sink but don't take my hand off it. "Uh-huh. Important how?"

Someone knocks on the door. "Open up, Miranda." It's Rhys.

"Give me a minute." I know I should include Rhys in the interrogation, but my patience is razor thin. I press the little lock button on the doorknob.

"Please?" he says. He knocks on the door again, softly this time. "Don't do anything stupid."

Ignoring him, I swivel back to the clone. "I said, *important how?*"

M-96 says, "I don't know—I swear! We're having a briefing very soon. In the Verge. Ninety minutes from now."

"Miranda, seriously, you have to come see this," Rhys says through the door.

"I'm coming." I put my hand on the doorknob. "What are you talking about? I destroyed the Verge."

She doesn't say anything.

Rhys twists the doorknob so hard the lock button pops out. He opens the door. "You *really* need to see this."

I think I already know what he wants to show me. "I'm not done with you," I say to M-96. She nods rapidly, so obedient I almost want to pat her on the head. I give her restraints a final once-over; everything's secure.

In the main room, Sophia is huddled in a blanket on the couch. Her dark skin is flushed, and tears glaze her cheeks. She jerks her chin to the broken window, where Noble is staring out.

I walk up next to him in time to see the Verge taking

shape. The metal disk in the park is no longer flat. It's telescoping upward, like a mountain rising from the earth, each level smaller in diameter than the last, until the building takes on the shape of a metallic beehive.

There is one difference from the Verge I destroyed, though. This one has a huge column at the very top, not an office. As we watch, the top of the column begins to glow red. It becomes too bright to look at. Just before I turn away, it fires a thick red beam straight up into the sky. My eyes follow the beam to the clouds, where a plane is flying over the city. The plane is just a white speck, a long gray contrail behind it. A military spy plane, if I had to guess, since air traffic has probably been grounded by now. The beam hits the plane, turning it into a ball of red light that soon becomes chunks of fiery debris. The pieces rain down around Manhattan, taking an eternity to fall, like sparks from some kind of horrific firework.

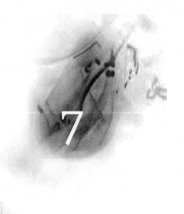

7

"We have two options," I say. "Rhys and I can take their uniforms and go to this briefing in the Verge, or we can track down Peter and see if he's connected with whatever armed forces are in the city."

Secretly, I hope we don't see Peter for a while. Much as I want him fighting by my side, I hope he's lying low, waiting for things to settle down. Traveling alone will be a risk once enough people start to recognize the other Peters out there.

Stay safe, I think, as hard as I can, but I'm no telepath.

We're in the kitchen. R-34 is still passed out, and M-96 knows she's already on two strikes. I checked on her a minute ago, and she was in the same position, watching me like a wounded animal. I'm a little disgusted she was cowed so easily.

"I think we'd better do both," Noble replies.

"What do we do with the clones?" Rhys says.

Noble frowns, scratching his beard. "They're not going anywhere. We can secure them further, and you've already illustrated what will happen if they use their powers again."

Sophia walks over. She lets her blanket fall to the floor. "Noble and I can look for Peter. Maybe we can rendezvous somewhere tonight."

"Look for him *where*?" I ask. "It's not a small city."

"We have other safe houses," Noble says. "We'll start there."

"They clearly have your description," I say. "Or else Thing One and Thing Two over here wouldn't have freaked out. And the army is scanning anyone they come across."

Sophia smiles, and I daresay there's some condescension in it. "Miranda, no offense, but Noble and I learned how to stay out of sight a long time ago."

"And we won't be completely helpless in terms of weaponry," Noble says, putting his hand on my shoulder. "But thank you for your concern." He gives me a comforting, fatherly grin.

Rhys looks at me. "We should go, Mir."

I nod. "Fine." My heart wants to look for Peter with Noble and Sophia, but I know getting into the Verge is more important. Priority one is to find out if True Earth is really just here for East, or if they've come back to finish the job of killing every single human on the planet. I have a sneaking suspicion they're not just going to take their ball and go home.

"Stay out of the subway, no matter where you have to go," I say to Noble and Sophia. "True Earth has new monsters. Not eyeless."

Sophia frowns. "Do I even want to know?"

"No," Rhys says. "Trust me."

I leave everyone in the kitchen and go back to the bathroom as Rhys begins to explain the spiders anyway. M-96 is staring at a spot on the floor. I put my foot on her chair and push down until it's upright.

"Are you going to use your power?" I say.

She shakes her head.

"Say it."

"No," she says.

"Good." I give her a smile. "I need your suit."

Her upper lip curls slightly. "You'll get me in trouble."

"Do you really think you have a choice?" She holds still while I remove the suit from her, never freeing more than one of her limbs at a time. Underneath she wears some kind of thin jumpsuit. A muscle in her forearm begins to spasm; I can feel how badly she wants to hurt me. But she's smarter than that.

"Tell me how the ranks work," I say as I double-check her restraints. "What color suit means what? I want details."

She sighs, angling her lip so it blows hair off her forehead.

"At the top are the blue suits. There are thirty of them. Below that is silver, who are captains. Then comes us, the reds, the specialists. Black or white armor are for the grunts. Satisfied?"

"What's a specialist?"

She grins. "For this mission, we control the H10."

A chill runs up and down my spine. H9 is a kind of plastic explosive that does less exploding and more melting with anything it touches. Last summer we used lots of it to destroy the creators' main lab in Cleveland. I'm assuming H10 is some kind of variant.

She must sense I'm about to ask more questions. "Look, just go to the briefing and you'll find out what you're supposed to do. We're using it on buildings we suspect might hold East. It's simple."

"What does East have that you want?"

"I told you, I don't know. We were going to find out tonight, until you attacked us."

The audacity of that statement makes my mouth fall open— *we* attacked *them*? I mean, yes, we did, but can one really attack *invaders*? M-96 is about to laugh, but I shove her in the chest again and she slams backward onto the tub. This time the chair kicks out and she falls flat on her back.

I take the suit into Peter's room. I know it's his because there's a picture of me on his nightstand. I don't remember the picture being taken. I'm in our old kitchen, face half turned away, my hair hanging in front of my right eye. It looks like I was posing, but I wasn't.

I shut the door behind me, then strip out of my suit. I lay it on the bed, next to M-96's red one, then sprawl on the comforter. I can smell Peter in the pillow, and my eyes prick with tears. We agreed to talk after we saved the world. I promised him, even though I knew I was going to die. Now I'm back, and he's not here, and I have no idea what he'll think of it all. Am I the same person to him? Does it matter how many times I come back? It has to.

It's wrong, but I go through Peter's drawers. I find random clothes that aren't folded. An old T-shirt I used to wear to bed. On his dresser, disassembled guns are lined up nice and neat, freshly oiled. In his closet are a spare scaled suit and a set of military fatigues. I consider taking the sword I find on the top shelf, since I don't feel right using M-96's, but I think I'll get used to Beacon's new hilt. We've been through a lot together, me and Beacon, and the blade seems whole, which is what matters.

Someone knocks on the door, and before I can say anything it opens. "Hey—Oh my God!" Rhys says, slapping a hand over his eyes.

I jump into the closet. "Most people wait for a response after knocking!"

"I'm sorry! I just— It's getting late! And..."

"Turn around!"

He does. I creep over to the bed, then pull on the red suit of armor. It feels no different from my suit. The scales are a deep red, like half-dried blood.

"Okay," I say.

He turns around, cheeks flushed. "I didn't see anything. I saw a little bit. Not much really at all, I would say. Hey, you were the one standing around naked like a weirdo."

"Uh-huh. Let's get on with it. You need to put on R-34's suit too."

"Yeah, um. I was about to ask you for help. I just feel weird . . . undressing myself."

"Rhys. You undress yourself every day. At least I hope you do."

"Right, but it's me! He's him. But me. I—please?"

I can't help but smile. "Okay, let's go."

R-34 is awake when we come out of the bedroom. He sees my suit and the badge under my throat. His eyes go wide, and he grits his teeth. "Ninety-six, where are you?" he calls.

"In here," she says from the bathroom. "Don't do anything stupid." Rhys said the same thing to me only a few minutes ago.

Rhys goes through the same process I did of removing R-34's suit, and I help, keeping a firm grip on whatever limb is free at the moment. "Sorry about this, pal," Rhys says. "Hey, what do you call that cool car of yours we stole?"

"We call them..." He doesn't finish, as if he just remembered he's not supposed to volunteer information.

"Do we really have to go through this every time we ask a question?" I say.

"*Thorns*. They're called Thorns."

Rhys and I share a look, and then we burst out laughing.

"Thorns..." I barely get it out. "Roses..."

Our laughter catches. Noble starts laughing over his maps. Sophia is giggling on the couch. R-34 is looking at the floor. I can't stop; I can't breathe. Tears are streaming down my face. It's not even that funny, or funny at all, now that I think about it, but I can feel the tension coming out of me in waves.

Rhys speaks between gasps. "You guys—are so lame."

R-34's cheeks are red. "I didn't come up with the name."

Slowly, we get ourselves under control. It felt good to laugh, but now the absence of that laughter is almost painful.

"All right," Rhys says, wiping a tear away. "So what are those jets called? Stamens?" He laughs again, but there's no feeling behind it this time. The moment has passed.

"They have some technical name, but we call them Axes. Because they're flat and rectangular, like an ax. Is that funny?"

Maybe, but I'm done laughing.

"And the weapons?" I say.

R-34 continues while Rhys slips into his armor. "We call the rifles RAWs—Rose Assault Weapons. They fire iridium rounds that transfer their kinetic energy to the target without going through them, essentially vaporizing the target, depending on the material. If you accidentally shoot yourself on max power, you will die." He takes a shuddering breath. "Each RAW is coded to our armor. If you're not wearing it, you can't fire one."

"Why don't you tell them everything!" M-96 shouts from the bathroom.

"I'm trying to keep us alive!" he shouts back.

"You're doing a good job," I tell him.

We do a last-minute check. Rhys looks good in red. He shakes Noble's hand, but Noble pulls him into a hug. They pat each other on the back a few times like guys do. "Got a plan?" Rhys says.

"Oh yes," Noble replies. "I plotted a course through the city that should keep us off the main avenues. If Peter's hiding, we'll find him."

Sophia hugs me again. "I'm glad you're back. Being the only girl around here..."

"Sucks," Rhys offers.

"Yes," Sophia says. "Very much." But she smiles to show it doesn't really.

"I'm glad I'm back too," I reply, though technically the jury is still out on that one. I guess I can't be mad I'm alive. "You feeling okay now?"

She sniffs. "Yeah. Thanks for not letting me fall to my death. I won't let them catch me off guard again."

If only she could control it. I nod anyway.

Noble gives us earpieces small enough to be nearly invisible. "Touch these to activate them. Don't use them inside the Verge, in case they're tracking radio frequencies. After you're out, check in with us to see what's going on."

"Will do," Rhys says.

"Is there anything you can tell us about East?" I ask him.

Noble scratches his beard again. He shrugs. "I haven't seen him in years. For what it's worth, he . . . was one of the good ones. If any of us were good. I don't know what he's been up to, but I know he left the creators, of his own volition, sometime after I did. I'd thought they killed him, but . . ."

"Apparently not," Rhys finishes.

"Apparently," Noble says, clapping Rhys on the shoulder. "Clear eyes out there. And keep an eye on him, Miranda. Actually, use two."

"Yes, sir," we reply in unison.

We get into the elevator. Noble and Sophia watch us, and I can tell Sophia wants to say something to Rhys, but she only bites her lower lip, nods, and turns away. Noble's holding the shotgun, which makes me feel better.

R-34 is watching us too. "Good luck," he says with a smirk.

On the way down, I nudge Rhys with my elbow. "I don't

know what I've missed, but if you don't tell Sophia how you feel, I will." It's a gamble, but I think I'm right.

Rhys is silent for ten floors. Then he sighs. "I will. When this is over, I will." He nudges me back. "And don't you threaten me. Sheesh, back for a few hours and already so demanding."

All circumstances aside, it's good to be back with Rhys.

In the garage, Rhys grabs the two RAWs from the Thorn. "Want to take the Thorn?" he says. He hands me one of the RAWs, which is long and boxy. There's a numbered dial on the side, I'm assuming for the power of each shot. Right now it's at five. Curious what a five does, I aim it at the far wall, tuck it up tight against my body, and pull the trigger.

The far wall *explodes*.

Chunks of rock rain down on the cars parked next to it. The depression is ten feet wide. There was no recoil, and the only sound was a loud hiss, which is strange because the bullet had to break the sound barrier to cause that much damage.

"Maybe don't do that again," Rhys says.

"At least now I know what it'll do." I turn the dial down to three. I imagine shooting an actual human body with this, and immediately regret it.

We stick the RAWs on our backs next to our blades, then walk up the ramp onto 60th Street, into a blisteringly cold afternoon. My face is instantly numb, but at least the snow has stopped. Automatically I look around for Peter, as if he's just going to be there on the street waiting. Wishful thinking.

The street is dead now, like an empty movie set, just a few extras loitering in the distance. Only the howl of the wind to keep us company. Most people have probably found shelter by now, but it feels temporary, as if everyone is waiting to see what happens next. I look up at the windows all around us and see faces looking down. People pointing, people taking note of our presence. We need to keep moving.

The air is clogged with smoke, along with a fine white powder—pulverized concrete from the initial attack, no doubt. Probably not safe to breathe, which is about the fortieth most important thing to think about right now.

Someone steps out of the coffee shop across the street, sees us, then steps back inside.

"We don't look like friendlies," I remind Rhys.

"No kidding," he says.

We cross the street and step into the park a few seconds later. A path has been carved through the snow. Through the trees I hear the strange tones put out by the Thorns as they patrol the area.

"So Noble is pretty awesome," I say, fishing a little. When I died, Rhys and Noble were just reconnecting after years apart.

He considers that for a moment. "Yeah, he is awesome. We're bonding, you know, that whole thing."

"No, I don't know how one clone bonds with another clone." I tried once, with Sequel, before she was replaced with the homicidal maniac that killed Noah.

Rhys gives a halfhearted chuckle. "Yeah, well, I don't think it will ever be normal. But I gotta say, having him around is great. He's like a..."

"Father?"

He nods. "The closest I'll ever have."

"That goes for me too," I add.

A hundred yards later we come across our first Rose. It's a Peter, wearing a white suit that seems pure and angelic against the grayish snow. His badge says P-908. Seeing the clone's blue eyes is enough to make me feel sick. Last time I saw my Peter, his eyes had deepened to purple from using the memory band.

P-908 seems to stiffen when he sees us, then he nods. We nod back and keep moving.

"Stay casual," I say.

We enter a scorched section of the park. Limbless black trunks jut out of the ground like spikes. Ahead a Thorn rushes by from left to right, plowing through the trees like they're matchsticks. We come across more Roses armed with RAWs and heading out of the park. They either nod or ignore us. Thank goodness for the red suits.

My eyes dart from trunk to trunk, and I realize I'm not looking for Roses. I'm looking for those spiders. On open ground, we'd be dead meat. What kind of sick mind can not only dream up a creature like that, but also create it?

After a thick clot of trees, the Verge comes into view. It's larger than Commander Gane's had been, as wide as any skyscraper, but squat like a beehive. I can feel some kind of power radiating off of it. Without warning, the top begins to glow bright red again, followed by a sound so loud my teeth vibrate. I have to shield my eyes. When I look skyward, I can just see a hole the laser burned through the cloud cover and blue sky beyond.

Through it is a blot of smoke, no larger than a pebble held at arm's length. Another spy plane, or maybe they got smart and started using satellites. The rage I feel is the worst kind—helpless. I might as well be standing in the sun on a summer day, my skin is so hot.

Rhys gives my hand a squeeze and we keep moving, because we have to. The entrance to the Verge is straight ahead.

I will burn this place to the ground, I think as we step inside.

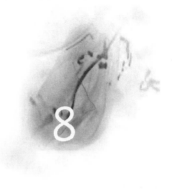

8

Inside, the Verge is identical to the one I died in, as far as I can tell. The levels are circular and overlook the open interior, with branching walkways connected to a pillar in the middle, which starts on the second level, supported by four extending bridges, like spokes on a wheel. As we walk in there's a little kiosk with a screen that says TYPE IN YOUR NUMBER.

Beyond that, the Black takes up most of the floor. Roses continue to pull themselves out of it, like animals freeing themselves from a tar pit. A siren blows, and the Roses scatter away from the hole, the two cranes mounted on the floor swinging out of the way. Two seconds later, an Ax bursts out of the

Black, filling the air with noise and heat and wind. The four engines in the corners of the plane spit down bluish-green fire, and the heat forces me to put a hand over my face. It flies forward, exiting through a large door on the other side of the Verge.

Two more Axes come out of the hole in rapid succession. Then the cranes go to work pulling Thorns out of the Black. Each Thorn is already loaded with Roses, who immediately drive them out of the Verge and into the park.

Rhys and I are just standing here, mesmerized, watching as the invasion force bubbles up from a hole in the ground. It's all very efficient. I'm sure they're so proud.

"C'mon," I say, tugging him forward once the siren stops. More Roses are climbing out of the hole now that it's clear. We walk up to the kiosk. I type in *M-96* and hit ENTER. The screen immediately comes back with TEAM 16, LEVEL 9, DORM 16.

"Let me make sure we're in the same room," Rhys says, typing in his number. It comes back the same, thankfully.

We skirt around the circumference of the Verge until we come to a set of stairs. The stairs rise over the Black and lead to elevator doors located at the bottom of the pillar.

The silent black circle is now directly below us. I wonder what would happen if I fell through.

"I don't get it," Rhys says, looking around. "How can they have a briefing here? There's no room."

"I don't know," I say as we step into the elevator. "And they wouldn't recall everyone in the city just for a meeting."

"Level," the elevator says.

"Nine," I reply.

We rise for a few seconds, and the doors open on another catwalk. Three Roses—a P, R, and N—are waiting to get in. The P and N are in silver armor. I nod to them and they ignore me. The circumference of level nine, and all the levels, probably, is ringed by dorm rooms. We find the one labeled 16. A device built into the door scans the badges on our chests, and then the door slides open.

It's just like home. Bunk beds on both sides. Dressers, a fridge, a bathroom. It's so familiar it hurts.

At the table in the middle of the room sit an Olive, a Noah, and a Peter. The other members of my team are right here in front of me, but of course they aren't actually mine. Two of my real Alpha teammates are dead, and Peter is who knows where. But I wouldn't know the difference just by looking at this team, at least not at first glance. The Peter's eyes hold a familiar light, and the Olive's posture is the same as I remember.

The Peter leans around the Noah to look at us. "Finally. Where have you guys been?"

We step into the room, and the door closes behind us. An excruciating second passes where Rhys and I wait for each other to say something first.

"Uh," Rhys says. A good start.

The Noah and the Peter are wearing black, the Olive white, which means we're ranked above them. So we won't have to answer any awkward questions. And if we're different ranks, maybe that means the team hasn't been training together from the start. M-96 and R-34 could be strangers. I hope.

"Don't worry about it," I say.

The Peter and the Noah share a look, like *What's her deal?* I read their badges quickly while their eyes are on each other—O-9, P-230, and N-7.

N-7 leans back in his chair and tosses some playing cards onto the table. Their fellow Roses are outside destroying our city, and they're playing *cards*. "No, really, where have you been? We were supposed to be on mission twenty-five minutes ago."

Rhys and I are still standing at the other end of the room, which has to look weird. I move forward and sit down at the table. Rhys follows. The three of them wait for us to elaborate.

"We got held up," Rhys says.

"I thought the briefing is coming up," I say. Instantly I know it sounds stupid. Wouldn't I know what we're supposed to be doing?

Olive raises her eyebrow at Noah. "Are you guys feeling okay?"

I shake my head, trying to recover. "No, not really. A few citizens were unruly, and Thirty-four had to put them down."

"Put them down," P-230 repeats.

"Yes," I say, feeling my cheeks flush with heat. Does that phrase sound out of place to them? I have no idea if I'm making things worse or not. "Haven't you been outside? It's insane."

"*No*," N-7 says. "You *told* us to stay put. We've been waiting for you to come back."

"Not long, though," O-9 says, shooting Noah a look that I've seen before. The one that says *Shut your mouth before it gets you in trouble*. "We just got here."

"My weapon was faulty," P-230 says. "I asked everyone to wait while I went to the armory."

Rhys stands up. "Well, then, let's get to it." A bead of sweat appears at his hairline.

"Great," N-7 says, clearly exasperated.

The three Roses stand in unison and gather their weapons. Rhys and I share a look, and I know he's feeling the same kind of dread I am. We have no idea what we're doing, and they're going to find out sooner or later. Right now all we can do is roll with it.

We leave the dorm and head back to the elevator, passing several other teams along the way.

"Where'd you park the Thorn?" O-9 asks Rhys.

"I left it on the street," Rhys says plainly.

O-9 actually gasps.

"Relax," Rhys says, and I can tell he's thinking fast. "I wanted to maintain a presence out there even though we had to leave. Some citizens were gathering, but the Thorns scare them."

"Good thinking," P-230 says. Rhys almost smiles at me.

Something vibrates against my left forearm. Everyone stops, which means they must feel it too. I twist my hand palm-up, and words scroll across the scales on my forearm.

BRIEFING CANCELED

FUGITIVE SIGHTED BETWEEN AVENUES SEVEN AND EIGHT

BETWEEN 50TH STREET AND 59TH STREET

AS OF NINETY SECONDS AGO

PERIMETER BEING ESTABLISHED

CONSIDER EXTREMELY DANGEROUS

THOUGHT TO POSSESS THE KEY

TEAMS 3, 4, 9, 16: REPORT TO THIS LOCATION

ALL OTHER TEAMS MAINTAIN PERIMETER

Team 16, that's us. Two seconds pass, then another sentence scrolls across my arm, one that makes the hair on the back of my neck stand up.

CONFIRMED: FUGITIVE HAS POSSESSION OF THE KEY

"Wow," O-9 says. "We might be going home sooner than expected."

"I can't believe we're on," N-7 says, shifting from foot to foot. "What the hell is the Key? Why don't they tell us these things?"

"It's a rush job," O-9 says. "I heard a rumor the director lost something very important. *Extremely* important."

N-7 smirks. "Like when she lost the Torch?"

O-9's eyes go wide with that *Shut up, you idiot* look again.

P-230 puts his hand on my shoulder. "That means you need to get your Thorn. Now. We'll take an Ax and meet you there."

I nod, trying to not make it seem like this is the greatest idea I've ever heard. We all take the elevator down, and Rhys and I split away from our team without so much as a good-bye. A minute later we're sprinting across Central Park, back toward the garage. On both sides of us, Thorns scream away to the south, kicking up big trails of snow with their knobby tires. Overhead, Axes race across the sky. They're coming from all over the city.

Rhys and I run flat out. I don't know what the Key is, but I know True Earth possessing it can't be good.

We make it back to the garage out of breath but warmed up. My legs are shaking—from the adrenaline, I hope. I can't afford to be weak, even if I did just get out of a tank.

"I'll drive." I touch the door on the driver's side, and it slides up into the frame. Rhys and I pile in, he presses a red button on the dash, and the Thorn hums to life. The console has a screen showing a map with live data of other vehicles in the city, which makes me realize the Roses could've tracked this thing right to Noble and Sophia. Wish we had noticed that earlier. Lucky for us, they had bigger things to worry about, and right now there are no other vehicles nearby. The Thorns, marked as red dots, and the Axes, marked in blue, swarm around the city like bees.

I give the Thorn some gas—or whatever this thing runs on—and it shoots forward, crushing a Mercedes and a Bentley that were parked in the two spaces in front of us. We barely feel the impact.

"Nice," Rhys says.

"It's touchy."

I reverse, then roar up the ramp and onto the street. I turn south on Broadway. Ahead and above, a cluster of Axes is spraying down an apartment building with a strange liquid. The bricks and windows are glossy with it, like they're covered in sap. On ground level, underdressed people are pouring out of the building's doors, only to be herded by Roses brandishing RAWs and swords. I feel faint pulses of fear rolling off the Roses, enough to subdue the people, to keep them from trying anything stupid but not enough to make them panic. The Roses on the street have formed a perimeter with the Thorns and are standing on top of them, firing nets down at the trapped people.

"What are they doing?" Rhys says.

The liquid covering the building ignites in the next second, fire so bright I have to look away. When my eyes adjust, the building is collapsing inward, melting into a puddle, like it was made of snow. I hit the gas without thinking.

"Miranda, no. No!" Rhys says when he can tell I'm speeding up to ram the nearest Thorn in front of us. "We need to stay undercover! We're in a good position!"

He punches me in the arm, hard. I lift my foot off the pedal and the Thorn's whine drops away. Anger dissolves into shame—I almost ruined everything on a knee-jerk reaction.

"What the hell was that?" he says.

"I'm sorry."

"I'm driving next time."

The other Thorns are backing out of there as the molten remains of the building leak onto the street. Three Axes swoop in, using their downward thrust to knock over the few people who managed to flee. The Roses swoop in and begin scanning people before they can stand up again.

I slam to a stop outside the perimeter, and no one spares me a passing glance. We get out of the Thorn and walk over to the ring of Roses. The tenants of the building are jammed in the middle, clearly terrified out of their minds. The weak fear waves I felt before are stronger the closer I get, an itch I feel on the inside of my skull. The urge to release my own waves is strong and fills me with disgust. An automatic reaction, a kind of pack mentality built into my brain, I guess. I dismiss it, leaving the itch unscratched.

The people are reduced to a clump of miserable, sobbing humans. The Roses sit them down right there on the icy street. There's not a thing I can do for them right now. I just have to sit there and feel their fear.

And then the director shows up.

9

The director jumps off a nearby Ax that's hovering twenty feet off the ground. She falls into a forward roll and pops up like she didn't just leap off a jet. Adrenaline hits my bloodstream, a punch to the stomach that sets my legs trembling again.

My fingers go to the RAW on my back. I even get my hand closed around it. I'll spin the dial up to ten, then fire right between her eyes. But a strong hand grabs my wrist, squeezing until I let go. It's not Rhys, because he's staring straight ahead at the director, with his mouth slightly open. I turn my head and see Olivia.

The Original Olivia, one of the Ruling Five, dressed in her golden armor polished to a mirror finish. It has to be her. This is the woman who has lived for a thousand years. She has the same almond eyes, pale skin, and midnight hair as my friend Olive did, before she was killed. She stopped me from grabbing my RAW but didn't make a scene, or even eye contact.

"Don't," she whispers, then releases me and walks to the director. An elderly man cowers away from her, falling against a woman. His khakis are wet with urine. He's terrified, and not from psychic waves. Just good old-fashioned fear; I can taste the difference somehow. It makes me sick to my stomach. This guy didn't wake up this morning thinking he was going to be so scared he'd piss himself.

My hand is on the RAW again, but I don't pull it. I know I need to give Olivia a chance to do something, *anything*. I force myself to let go of the grip a second time, exhaling slowly as I do.

"Is one among you Noah East?" the director calls out. Her hair is golden, not auburn like every other Miranda. The light is gray and fading, but the scales of her suit still shine like Olivia's.

Olivia and the director begin circling the group of people. Behind them, a pair of Axes hover over the molten wreckage of the building, scanning with lasers that sweep back and forth. The air is sharp and bitter with chemicals and smoke.

The people stay silent. Just a whimper here or there.

The director confers with a nearby Rhys wearing silver

armor. The Rhys goes into the crowd and pulls out a short balding man wearing a coat too light for the weather. His breath comes out in short, machine-gun-like puffs.

I creep closer. Rhys reaches to grab my arm, but I move out of the way.

"Why did you say the fugitive was here?" the director asks the man.

The man trips over his words. "I'm sorry. I'm sorry. I—I—I thought I saw him. I wanted you to have what you wanted. Please. My family."

The director clenches her jaw. "You've wasted my time."

"I'm sorry! I—"

The director punches him so hard in the face I hear his cheek crack. He drops straight down to his knees, then onto his side, one foot twitching. Everyone starts screaming, but the screams turns to whimpers as the Roses deliver a short fear wave meant to subdue.

This is madness. What am I even doing here if I'm just going to let people die? But even if I shoot the director dead, she'd just come back in another body. Her identity is saved in several different places—where, I have no idea—and constantly updated. I could never really kill her. Meanwhile I would die for nothing.

Again.

"This is what happens when you waste our time," she tells

the cowering people. "Go to Central Park. We have a shelter there." The people don't move right away, and I feel the director give off a short, hard burst of fear. The people scream and trip over themselves and take off up Broadway toward the park.

The director notices all the Roses standing around. "Back to work!" she yells.

"You heard her," Olivia says. Her eyes settle on me, then flit away.

The Roses walk back to their Thorns, then drive to wherever they're supposed to go.

My arm buzzes with a new order.

TEAM 16 REQUESTS COMM CHECK

N-7: M-96 & R-34—WHY DON'T YOU HAVE YOUR EARPIECES IN?

O-9: WE CAN HEAR EACH OTHER. CAN YOU HEAR US?

I stare at the words on my arm for a full two seconds, my heart pounding again.

Rhys is reading his arm too. "Oh my God," he says. "The Roses have some kind of hidden communications gear."

I look up and the director is gone. Olivia is climbing into her Thorn across the street.

Our "team" has been trying to get in contact with us, yet the captured Roses in our apartment haven't told on us. Why?

I tap my ear to activate the comm Noble gave me. There's a click to let me know the channel is open, followed by the hiss of open air at the other end. "Noble. Noble, are you there?"

No response.

Olivia starts her Thorn across the street. She looks at me again. It's an invitation. The only Roses nearby are the ones walking around on the steaming ruins of the building, looking for something—the Key, presumably.

I grab Rhys's arm. "You have to go back and make sure Noble and Sophia are safe."

He nods sharply. "I'm on it. Where are you going?"

I'm already walking across the street. "To find out what the hell is going on."

10

Olivia tracks me through the windshield as I walk around the front of the Thorn. I scan the area quickly, but no one seems to be watching. Every citizen in the immediate area has split.

The passenger door slides up, and I fall into the seat. The blast of heat is glorious. I almost feel like a real person again.

Olivia starts driving without a word. We plow through the giant cloud of steam lingering in the street.

"That was very stupid, what I stopped you from doing."

"Then it's a good thing you stopped me," I reply. "How did you know it was me?"

She gives me a look like, *Please, do you know who I am?* "I'm sorry. I'm sorry your sacrifice didn't buy more time. I thought it would." But she says it like she knew it wouldn't. "It must have been an unpleasant experience."

"I barely felt it," I say, because it's true. Just that brief pain, then nothing, and even the memory of the pain is fading. Maybe my mind is trying to protect itself.

Now that the initial assault seems to be over, pedestrians have appeared again, though the streets still feel half empty. Every eye is on the Thorn as we pass. People have armfuls of stuff—clothes, food, whatever they can carry. A few of the stupider ones are carrying electronics.

The streets are still clogged with abandoned cars, but Olivia swerves around them, or plows right through, wedging the cars aside. A FreshDirect delivery van has been completely gutted, the boxes torn open and emptied, vegetables smashed in the snow.

"What can I do for you?" Olivia says.

"I need to know what the Key is."

She turns into a parking garage and drives right through the gate, snapping it off. We cruise up and around a few levels, fast, until Olivia slides into a spot.

She sits with both hands on the wheel for a moment. "Your world is about to change."

"You don't say."

She shakes her head. "I haven't been honest with you. From the beginning."

I feel a pang deep in my stomach, the kind you get when you know bad news is imminent, but you can't even guess what it is.

Olivia lets the seconds tick away.

"Tell me."

She sighs through her nose. "I can't just yet. Because I don't know what telling you will do."

"Okaayyyy." Tick tick tick. "You have to tell me something."

A muscle in her jaw twitches. "I can't tell you what to do next, and I can't stop you. I can only offer a bit of guidance."

"What have you been lying about?" The heat is stifling inside the Thorn now, and I feel like I'm going to throw up. "Tell me. You have to tell me."

She ignores me. "I don't think you should fight back this time."

"Excuse me?"

A car door opens and closes on our level, then I hear an engine starting sluggishly in the cold. I watch out the back window as a car creeps by. When the driver spots the Thorn he peels out around the corner.

"True Earth is here to do a very specific thing. And stopping that thing might end this world for good."

"So now you're saying they want to *save us*?"

Olivia nods. "We're here to release the Black into your

world. It will no longer be a buffer between universes—it will be a part of your reality."

"Which means what?" My mouth is sticky with fear; I can't swallow.

"Releasing the Black into your world would re-create an event that we erased by accident."

"You're not making any sense."

"Listen. I helped you in the beginning because I wanted to prevent something awful from happening, something only I knew about. Something I couldn't share with the other Originals."

"Which is what?"

She still won't look at me directly. "Before I tell you, you need to understand that this world, the world you live in, is not a different universe. It is the *past* of my world."

"Come again?"

Now she looks at me. "This world will eventually become True Earth, far in the future."

"Bullshit." My hands are shaking.

"It's true. When the director decided it was time to cull this world, I wanted to stop her—"

"Why didn't you just *tell her the truth*?"

"I couldn't."

"Why not?"

"Because I did something wrong!" She screams it. I've never heard her scream before. I've never heard *any* Olivia scream before. "The director knows the truth now. She knows what this world means for our future, for the future of True Earth. And, Miranda . . . if she doesn't win, it's going to be bad for *everyone*."

The silence in the Thorn is heavy.

Finally, I ask, "What did you do wrong?" She looks down at her lap and it hits me. This being who has existed for a thousand years is unsure of herself.

"I don't know what would've happened if the eyeless were allowed to consume this world. I don't think I can ever know. But I do know what happened after you stopped them. . . ."

"What?" It should be something good, but it sounds like it's going to be bad.

"I'll show you everything," she says quietly.

Olivia pulls out a mask like the one I've used many times before. It allows the wearer to experience memories a previous user has stored on the device. But this one has a strip of wires running off it, wires that lead to another mask.

"I will show you what you need to see. Just listen to my voice."

I slide the helmet on and close my eyes, waiting for the familiar sting as microscopic needles pierce my skull, but it never comes.

When I open my eyes, I'm seated at a table with three other Originals—Peter, Noah, and Rhys. They're all talking, but I can't hear them. I'm seeing through Olivia's eyes.

In the Thorn, Olivia says, "We had a meeting one day in September. I will never forget it. It was the day we decided to overthrow our own leadership. Once, we were not the Ruling Five. We were underlings to Miranda. She was the supreme ruler. And she was bad."

Shocking.

Olivia goes on to explain that during her journeys through the Black, she discovered a new world. But it wasn't an alternate universe . . . it was the past. It was our world. Our world and True Earth are the same place, just over a thousand years apart.

"The other three Originals and I wanted to remove the director from power," she says. "But the change in balance would've made us appear weak to other worlds like ours, ones highly advanced. So I came up with a plan based on my discovery. Only I didn't share what I'd learned with the others. I foolishly decided to take it into my own hands. . . . I thought I could change things myself."

The scene changes, and now we're in a school—a junior high school judging by the kids. We watch a young girl with auburn hair carry her books through a hallway. I recognize the girl. It's me. No one seems to notice Olivia is watching her—it's like Olivia is invisible.

A boy with short hair and dark eyes approaches the girl from the side, but she can't see him because her hair is in the way. He brushes it out of her face and she jumps, then smiles when she sees it's Noah. Slowly, she wraps her arms around his neck and looks up into his face. The way Noah smiles at the girl reminds me of how he used to smile at me.

But that can't be *me*; that isn't right. At that age, I wasn't in school—I was training with Alpha team.

"Is that the director?"

"Yes," Olivia says. "Back when she was living a normal life."

My heart starts to race. "Wait. Does that mean she's still out there? In her normal life? If this is the past of True Earth, then she's out there walking around right now."

"Yes..." Olivia says.

"Well, where is she? We can find her. We can stop this right now."

"No, we can't. I already had the director killed when she was a teenager."

"But you just said—" I begin.

"Just watch."

The scene changes again. We're on top of a building. It's pouring rain. There is a dead body on the ground far below, blood pooling under it and mixing with the rainwater, but I can't make out many details from this distance. Olivia turns her face to the rain, and I can feel the cold drops on my skin like it's happening inside the Thorn.

She keeps talking. "I replaced the teenage version of the director, the one who knew nothing of this, with a clone, one I could guide from a distance. And it worked. When I returned to True Earth, things had changed. I'd altered the entire history of True Earth, and my companions never knew any differently. The planet was stable. The director was a partner to us now, not a queen. We ruled together." She shows me snippets of images, of the five of them ruling side by side, of the golden landscape I remember from my brief visit to True Earth. I watch the citizens of True Earth firing rockets into a smoggy gray sky. When they explode, a golden wave spreads out, changing the color of the sky permanently. "It was like recording over a tape."

Her words wash over me like water. I feel like I'm dreaming. What an unnatural thing, for us to exist right now. She's stopped showing me images—I see only darkness.

"Changes happening here and now had affected the future, but the trouble was, some changes don't have as big an impact as others. And in the moment, there's no way to know what's important. Until you do it."

She sighs. "But I noticed things were beginning to deteriorate for True Earth. The unity was short-lived, and when it began to crumble, it was worse than before. I couldn't explain it to the others without admitting what I'd done—it was all my fault. I knew they'd never forgive me.

"Things got worse and worse, and eventually there was no unity. There were power grabs. There were secret wars."

Her voice is thick with emotion. And regret.

"So I went back again. To try again."

Something buzzes inside the car. I hear her take off the mask, and I do the same.

"I have to go," she says, looking at the readout on her arm.

"You promised you would tell me everything." I know I'm still missing something crucial. It's like a missing piece of lung.

"And I will. Just stay out of trouble."

She reaches into the pouch on her waist. The distrustful part of me, the part that will never, ever go away, tenses, preparing for the possibility of a weapon. Of course there is none, just a small disk, like the one adhered to the base of my skull.

She drops it into my palm. "Use this when you're in a quiet place, a *safe* place. Do you understand? It may disorient you—I don't know how much, or for how long."

I nod, staring at her bloodred eyes, like the ones I now have after using the machine. I was hoping I'd be able to keep my green ones for a while.

"Are the other Originals here?" I want to know how many enemies I have.

"No. They're busy trying to take control of a world in shambles before it's too late. We no longer control True Earth the way we did. Now, please, get out."

I actually listen to her without putting up a fight for once. But before I shut the door, I have to ask, "What will releasing the Black do? What happens if the director finds the Key and uses it? I mean, that'll affect True Earth, won't it? Hurting us hurts you."

The look in Olivia's eyes erases any leftover warmth from the Thorn. "Anyone who possesses the Key when they enter the Black will go to a specific room between universes. There they are able to control and direct the Black as they choose."

"You didn't answer my question." But I tattoo that information into my brain—possess Key, control Black.

Her grim expression somehow becomes more grim. "Upon releasing the Black there will be darkness. Few will survive. But in time, you will flourish again."

I try to wrap my mind around the idea of my genetic twin thinking—*You know what? Screw it, let's try again. We can just wipe most of their world out!* Did she come to that conclusion during dinner? While she was showering? Or perhaps over drinks with some friends. Does she even have friends?

"Why don't you do something?" I say very quietly.

"Because it needs to happen. It *all* needs to happen. Use the disk I gave you, and you will understand."

"What am I supposed to do in the meantime?"

"Stay alive," she says.

Olivia zooms down the ramps to the street, and I take the stairs, thinking about Keys and clones and the end of the world. It doesn't seem real. *It needs to happen,* she said. I rub my thumb over the disk in my pouch, wondering what it can possibly show me to convince me that this needs to happen, that many *need* to die. I don't buy it. For so long I thought she was on our side.

On the street, the wind is blowing, and darkness has fallen. At the nearest intersection, two cars are smashed together, their windshields frosted with snow. I jog to a truck that looks like it's in better shape, and get inside. The keys are still in the ignition. I start it up, then head in the general direction of "home."

Maybe they found Peter and everyone is there.

The idea is so good it hurts. I hold on to it, as if wanting it hard enough will make it real.

The mood in the apartment is semi-relaxed when I come out of the elevator, and I'm immediately filled with relief.

Rhys holds up his hands. "No worries. They handed their comm units over to Noble after we left. They've been very cooperative. Noble was out of contact because of some reception issues, but I've been in touch with him. True Earth is apparently scrambling various frequencies on the island."

"Where are the Roses?" I ask.

"Tied up in Noble's bedroom. They're not going anywhere."

"And Noble and Sophia? Peter?"

Rhys frowns. "Noble and Sophia are still looking for Peter."

I go to the sink and fill a glass with water, then hunt for food in the fridge. It's the only action I can think of to mask my disappointment.

"Don't worry about them," Rhys says. "Let's talk about the Verge. I . . . don't think we should go back."

"We've been out of contact for a long time, and our teammates were already suspicious," I say. "There's a good chance they'll apprehend us as soon as we enter the Verge."

"That's what I was thinking," he says, looking relieved.

"But we have to go anyway."

"What?"

I explain the Key to him, and what it means if the director gets her hands on it. This leads to more questions, and I tell him what Olivia told and showed me.

His already pale skin turns a cooler shade of gray. "I thought your eyes were a little red."

"The bottom line is we need to find the Key," I say, "then we can figure out what to do with it."

"But why do we have to let them release the Black? Why are we supposed to *let* it happen? Are you kidding me?"

"I don't know any more than what I told you."

"You're in a safe place. Why don't you use the disk now?"

"Because I don't know what it's going to do to me. Olivia said it'll disorient me, and she doesn't know for how long. Do you agree we need to find the Key more than anything else?"

"I agree," he says. "Let's do it."

I drink another glass of water in case there isn't water to drink later. "We're gonna need help. East could be anywhere. At least if the Roses find him and the Key before we do, being on the inside is the best chance we have of stealing it."

Rhys's eyes light up with an idea. "What if we just find the Originals as kids and kill them? Or beat 'em up or something. Olivia said the future is affected by changes in the past, right?"

"If you have an idea of where they are in the United States of America, that's great. Or if you have an idea of how to get off this island, even better. But I'm sure Olivia has them protected. Besides, if they die, what would that mean for us? We're going to have to trust Olivia until we know more. Though I use the word *trust* lightly."

He frowns. "What I don't get is, if the Originals are still here, living their lives before they became the Originals, then how could *we* have been here for years?"

"Because we're from True Earth ourselves. Right?"

He lets out a low sigh. "Man, all along we've been living in the same world as the people who will eventually create us in the future and bring us back to now. What a time to be alive!" He says it like a joke, but I can see how it makes him feel. Rhys can guard his eyes all he wants, but I see the pain behind them. To know you're not a person, you're a thing...

He's about to say more when a tinny noise comes from the countertop; I look for the source—two earpieces not so different from ours.

I take out Noble's earpiece and put the new one in.

I hear O-9's voice. "—back to the Verge. Getting some rack. P-230, any word yet?"

My heart jolts; O-9 doesn't sound alarmed, yet it's possible the team could've heard us speaking just now. A mistake. But Noble probably left the earpieces out knowing we would need them.

P-230 says, "Nothing."

"This is weird," O-9 replies.

"Guys," N-7 says. "Give them some time. Did you notice what color their suits are? It's not for us to decide."

"It's for a blue or silver suit, which is who I'm going to next if they stay off grid," O-9 says.

"Easy there," P-230 says.

"This is M-96," I say.

"See?" N-7 says.

"Where have you been?" O-9 demands.

"Excuse me?" I say. Rhys quickly fits his own earpiece in. I know exactly how I'm going to play this.

The silence on the channel stretches.

"We had comm issues, which we've rectified now. Do you have a problem?"

Another few seconds pass, then O-9 says, "No."

"Good. What is your status?"

"We're supposed to be on H10 duty as of fifteen minutes ago," P-230 says. "We're regrouping at the Verge. Seventeen new sightings of our target, all of which need to be confirmed."

N-7 actually laughs. "That's a lot of buildings to burn down."

P-230 says, "I don't know if this is the right play. These people are going to be angry if we keep turning their buildings into molten rock."

"We can control them," N-7 says. "Did you forget?"

"No, of course not. But do we really want to incite an organized rebellion?"

"Leave the strategizing for the blue suits," I say. "We'll meet you in the dorm."

I touch the piece in my ear and hear the channel go silent. "Hello?" I say, but there is no response. Rhys does the same.

Over Rhys's shoulder I can see the windows on the other

side of the apartment, the ones overlooking the Hudson. The glass thrums every few minutes as the attacks on the gun turrets start up again. The United States is lobbing missile after missile across the river, and the turrets are just shooting them out of the air. The Hudson is littered with floating pieces of wreckage. Parts of the river are on fire. Most of the lights in New Jersey are out, but it's probably a precaution, the way cities in Europe would turn out the lights in World War II to make it harder for enemy pilots to hit their targets.

I don't see any activity across the river—True Earth's quarry is here. For now, the rest of the world seems safe.

"Let's go," Rhys says after watching for a moment.

I follow him back into the cold. He'd parked the Thorn on the street, between two white box trucks. A little ways past, an ambulance sits with the flashers on, strobing the buildings with red. The EMTs eye us carefully while they tend to a few injured people.

A shiver of disgust runs through me. *I'm on your side,* I want to shout to them. *I just look like the bad guy.* Then I notice three Roses in black standing on the sidewalk, next to the ambulances, watching the EMTs with folded arms. The Noah with them turns his gaze toward us, but we get into the Thorn before he tries to signal. At least the Roses are letting us tend to the wounded.

Rhys drives us back to the Verge in silence. It's not until he's parked next to a copse of trees that he says, "Are you ready?"

I can taste the fear in my throat, but also the relief that comes with having no other choice. This is what we have to do, if we're going to have any chance.

"I guess we'll see."

Rhys puts his hand on top of mine, then curls his fingers around it. The scales from our suits scrape over one another.

"Whatever happens, you know. Blah blah blah, sentimental stuff."

I put my other hand on top of his. "I know, Rhys. Likewise."

We get out and enter the Verge. Rhys goes ahead of me so we're not together. We don't want to arouse suspicion. I stop to watch the cranes pull a Thorn from the Black, and then another. As soon as their wheels touch down, the Thorns launch from the Verge, adding to the city's chaos. Another Thorn rises from the darkness as I climb the stairs to the elevator.

The elevator doors open, revealing a Peter. P-81, more specifically. A black suit. I make eye contact, but not for long—I feel like the lie is all over my face, and, truth be told, I don't want to look at any Peter that isn't mine.

The Peter actually pauses midstep, and I think, *Oh God, he knows.*

But then he just moves past me, his shoulder brushing mine. "Excuse me," he says.

"Sorry," I say automatically, and he half turns back to me and does a kind of quick nod like, *No problemo*, before continuing on his way.

Did I just see...?

I watch the back of his head, hoping he turns around again, but he doesn't.

I stand there for ten more seconds, until someone else steps into the elevator. A different Rhys. "You coming?" he says.

"In a minute, thanks."

He raises an eyebrow, and the doors shut. The elevator hums as it rises. I look down at the ground level, but the Peter is gone.

I replay the moment again and again in my mind. His face. His eyes, which should have been bright blue, were a deeper shade, closer to purple.

And his chin...

The little white scar on his chin, just like the one on the Peter I call my own.

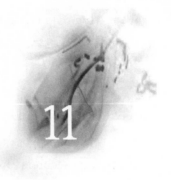

11

Stunned, I take the elevator to level nine. My face is flushed and my head is a little swimmy. Peter is here. It must've been him, even though now I'm trying to remember his chin, and it's a little blurry.... Could it be I just *wanted* it to be him? But no, he suspected it was me too, just from a look. That was his pause midstep—it had to be.

P-81. I have to find P-81.

When I get to the dorm, Rhys is talking to the others. N-7 nods at me.

"There you are," Rhys says. I must look distracted, because he gives me a weird look. "I was just talking about our comm issue. They sent up new earpieces for us."

"Hey," I say absently. *Get your mind in the game.* "Good. I have to go to the bathroom."

"Thanks for sharing," P-230 says as I walk past. I don't want to look at him right now.

In the bathroom I splash water on my face, then look at myself in the mirror. This cheek was never slashed open by Mrs. North's sword. The scar I'd gotten used to is gone. I touch the skin there anyway. There's a toothbrush wrapped in a plastic case with my number on it. I can't tell if it's been used or not, but I brush my teeth anyway for the first time since I came back. True Earth can't even spring for electric toothbrushes.

When I come out, my teammates are playing cards again, Rhys included. Olive is reading a hardcover book on her bunk. Where did she get it? Did they stop their patrol to rob a bookstore? The whole scene is strange to me. They go out and do whatever they're supposed to do—melt buildings, scan people, hurt people, whatever—and then come back and play cards to kill time? I want to scream *WHAT ARE YOU DOING?* at the top of my lungs.

"Schedule change," N-7 says to me. "We've got another hour before next patrol."

"We should sleep," P-230 says.

"*Should* is the key word there," N-7 replies.

They're just talking like nothing is happening. Before I was able to accept it as weird, but now it's a live wire touching my skin. I'm so angry my right hand starts shaking, so I ball it into a fist, then hide it behind my back. N-7 is eyeing me weirdly.

"I'll be back," I say, then march to the door before anyone can object. Really smooth. I shut the door behind me and press my back to the wall next to our room as clones walk by on my level. Two Mirandas carry a huge plastic tank with H10 labeled on the side. I want to make them drink it. Then, blessedly, I am by myself.

The door opens, and N-7 steps out. He looks both ways, as if checking to see if we're alone, and I stiffen. Before I know what's actually happening, he leans in and kisses me. I shove him away with both hands.

"Em, what are you doing?" he says. He isn't angry, more like astonished. He's breathing heavily, with these bewildered eyes, an expression I've never seen on the Noah I knew.

M-96 and N-7 must be "together," whatever that means for these people.

"You know, I didn't want to say anything, but you've been ridiculous since the promotion. You and Thirty-four both." His eyebrows go up. "What is it, we're not good enough for you now?"

There goes my hope that the team was unfamiliar with one another.

"I'm sorry." It sounds weak. I try to recover with, "Just not here."

"No, really, what was that? What's wrong with you?"

"There's nothing wrong with me." *I'm just in my third body that I know of, behind enemy lines with the two remaining members of my team, one of whom is unaccounted for.*

"I'm worried about you," he says softly. "You've been weird since we got here."

I believe him; the worry in his eyes is right there for me to see. Now he reminds me of the Noah I lost.

"I'm sorry. I'm sorry I've been acting differently."

My arm buzzes before he can reply. The display says NEXT PATROL: 52 MINUTES. REPORT TO QUARTERMASTER FOR H10 RESUPPLY.

"Come inside and talk to me," he says.

"No time," I say, holding up my arm to show him.

"Then later for sure. Promise me."

"Fine," I say, then start to walk away.

"Hang on, we'll go to the quartermaster together," he says.

I wave a hand. "I'll meet you there. I just want a minute alone." When I look over my shoulder, he's going back into the dorm. I feel a pang of guilt in my stomach for leaving Rhys, but I know he can handle himself.

I take the elevator back to the bottom level, then go up to the little kiosk. I type in *P-81.* The screen says TEAM 27,

LEVEL 12, DORM 12. My palms start sweating. A new copy of my Alpha team crawls out of the Black, all of them in white armor. They nod deferentially to me, then visit the kiosk while the Miranda on their team looks up their dorm number.

"This is exciting," the Olive says to me, and I almost throw her back into the Black.

I find myself standing in place again, feet rooted to the floor. If I'm right, then Peter would know I'd come looking for him. I could visit his dorm without too many questions being asked because my suit is red.

I make a decision and instantly feel better. I almost skip back to the elevator. *How observant are you, Peter?* I can't shake the feeling that he recognized me, that he *knew* me, even though the scar on my cheek is gone.

The elevator takes me to level twelve, and I find dorm twelve easily enough. The door is open. Inside is a dorm room identical to mine. Peter is sitting on his bed, hands on his knees. His head turns as I freeze in the doorway. We're alone.

"Can I help you?" he says, eyeing the badge on my chest. "You might have the wrong room."

"I..."

I'm too far away to see his chin.

"Yes?"

"P-81," I say, my voice so dry it comes out like a whisper. "P-81," I say again, stronger.

"That's my number, yes. Am I in trouble?"

I shut the door behind me. "No, nothing like that." I can feel my pulse thumping in my neck. I nod toward the bathroom. "Could you come with me?"

He's got his guard up, but I see the question in his eyes, the tiny sparkle of hope. His lips part. I pass him and walk into the bathroom. He follows cautiously, hands free and loose at his sides, ready to strike at a moment's notice.

"Is something wrong with my team?" he says.

I shut the door behind us and keep my hand on it. This is a gamble. Everything could be undone because of this. And it's not just me in danger here, but Rhys too. *Say you made a mistake. Leave. Wrong level, wrong dorm.*

"Why won't you answer me?" he says.

I turn to him.

I see the scar.

"You know me," I say.

He can't hide the reaction. Instantly he swallows hard and starts blinking, and his purple-blue eyes get shiny. He pretends to cough.

"Oh yeah?" he says. "I don't recognize your number." Still being cautious.

"Peter..." I say.

He lunges for me, but not to attack. His hands catch me under the arms and he lifts me up and I wrap my legs around his waist as my back hits the wall. His mouth crashes into mine so hard our teeth click and I taste blood from his lip, and then I feel wetness from his eyes on my cheeks. His legs are shaking, and he's pushing me against the wall so hard I can't breathe, but I don't want to breathe. What is breath, anyway?

We kiss for a long time. I don't know how long. I should probably know. But I don't care. Somehow his mouth tastes like spearmint, like the toothpaste I just used. At one point we don't move our lips, just keep them pressed together while we hold each other, breathing hard through our noses.

He pulls back to look into my eyes. "I knew it was you. At the elevator. I knew it. I don't know how, but I did." He swallows. "I'm sorry. I'm sorry you had to come back. It's not right."

Right now I am very glad to be alive.

"This is right."

He kisses me again, lightly. There is some blood on his upper lip. I wipe it away with my thumb and hold his face. I can feel his pulse under my hand, strong and steady, and the heat in his skin. There is a war outside and I don't want to fight it. I want to stay here, with him.

"This is dangerous," he says.

"I don't care. Where have you *been*?"

He shakes his head. "I'm sorry, I should've been there for you. But I saw an opening and I took it. I thought I could learn more on the inside."

"Have you?"

"Nothing that will help us win. The others have to be worried sick. I had twelve seconds to take this Peter's place. No time to let Noble know what I was doing. I tried using the radio later, and it was ja—"

I silence him with a kiss.

"They'll get over it."

I kiss him again. It doesn't matter now. He's here, alive.

But then I hear the door to room twelve hiss open.

We both hesitate, unsure of how to play it. Then I make a snap decision and shove him toward the door, while I slide into the farthest bathroom stall, one of three. The walls of the stall go from floor to ceiling. Peter grabs my arm again. He pulls me into a quick embrace and kisses me, hard and fast.

"Just in case," he whispers.

"Go!"

I shut the door as quietly as I can. The door has a gap in the bottom, about a foot tall, and anyone could see over the top if they jumped up. The toilet is filled with green liquid. I step onto the seat, lips buzzing from Peter's kiss. My breath sounds loud even through my nose. Outside the bathroom I hear Peter talking to someone. Casual voices, though I can't make out any words.

Two seconds later the bathroom door opens. I hear nearly silent feet against the floor, a rustle of hair—meaning it's either a Miranda or an Olive—and then nothing. For five whole seconds. The Rose has gone completely still. I hold my breath.

Then, a sniff.

The Rose is sniffing the air. I've been sweating, but I don't know if I smell. My hair doesn't hold a shampoo scent because I haven't showered since the tank. Maybe she's just been outside and has the sniffles.

My chest is burning red hot, so I exhale as quietly as possible. I can still hear it, though, and it sounds like I'm blowing out a tornado in the silence. I inhale long and slowly.

The Rose clears her throat, then goes into the stall right next to me. I hear her put the seat down, and then a few muted metallic sounds as she peels her suit away. After she finishes, she runs the sink and leaves.

I take another breath, wanting to collapse. It was so stupid to come here, yet I still can't regret it. Minutes pass while I wait for Peter to return, and I start getting antsy. I finally step off the seat and stretch.

Peter comes in a moment later. He doesn't say anything, just opens the stall door and wraps an arm around my waist and pulls me close.

"Who was it?"

"The Olive on my team. O-620. She actually seems okay, somehow."

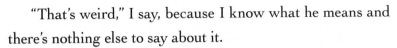

"That's weird," I say, because I know what he means and there's nothing else to say about it.

"You should leave now." He squeezes his arm a little tighter, pulling me closer. "Not that I want you to leave, because I definitely do not want that. But we'll meet up later."

"Of course. You'll be safe?"

He kisses me again instead of answering. His fingers find the seam in my suit at the top of my neck, but I catch his hands.

"Not if you want me to leave anytime soon," I say.

"I can't believe you're here." He's staring at me in wonder.

"Does it matter that I'm not the same?"

"No. It didn't matter the first time. Does it matter to you?"

"I wasn't sure before. But . . . now I'm happy." And I really mean it. Maybe I can look at this like another chance at life. My sacrifice doesn't have to be a waste, it can just be another step in this war. I *know* I'm not the same person. That person died in a horrible way, literally blown to pieces after getting torn apart by monsters, but . . . somehow I *am* her at the same time. I am me. I know this when I close my eyes.

"Good, I want you to stay happy. We need to find East and stop this. And then we're taking off, where no one can find us."

It sounds so good I actually shiver.

"I met with Olivia, the Original Olivia," I say, bringing us back to the task at hand. He needs to be briefed.

"I talked to her too, but not for long. She knew it was me. She told me what's happening, as far as what True Earth is trying to do here. She told me to be careful, but I'm not about to stop looking for the Key. We can't just let them do whatever they want. Not until we figure out what could happen."

"I'm worried. She's not telling us the whole story. Should we trust her?"

He shrugs. "I don't know. But she knows how to find us, and we're not in custody, so . . ."

I'm not convinced, but I'm not sure what else to do at the moment. So I just say, "Great. Then we'll save the day and get on with our lives."

"Exactly." His gaze falls for a second.

"What is it?"

He makes a sound that could possibly be a laugh. "I was mad at you. For a really long time. I was mad you took off like that and got all sacrificial without giving any of us a say."

"Peter, I'm—"

"No, listen. I'm not mad anymore. You being here reminds me of what matters."

"And what is that?"

"Life," he says.

He kisses me a final time, slowly, lingering, and then lifts his lips to kiss my forehead.

"Now go. We'll see each other soon."

Somehow I do it. I leave him behind. I don't look back on my way out of his room, because I know he'll be watching me, and if I look back I'll *go* back.

I leave level twelve and go down to my dorm, and when I open the door I see a person I don't recognize.

12

"**M**-96!" he says, like we're old friends.

He's wearing our armor, but he is not a Rose.

"Yes," I reply.

Everyone is staring at me in the doorway.

"Wonderful to meet you. My name is Albin."

His hair is medium length and mouse brown, combed straight back. He's smiling, and he's got two dimples in his cheeks, and bright white teeth. His eyes are warm, a brown so light it's honey, but bloodshot, like he's been up all night drinking. The scales on his armor are the color of plums, and there aren't any visible weapons on his person. His badge just has the letter *A* on it, no number.

"Hi, Albin."

He hasn't broken eye contact. My teammates are alternating looks between us. Something is very, very wrong.

"How can I help you?" I do my best to stand tall. Seeing Peter gave me new strength that I draw on right now.

"Oh, I'm very happy you said that," he says. "You can help me a great deal, so it's good you're in a helpful mood."

Rhys is standing behind everyone, but I can tell his chest is expanding and contracting faster than normal. He gives me a slight shake of his head—*Don't blow our cover just yet.*

Albin stares at me a beat too long, and then inhales quickly, like he just realized he should get on with it.

"Would you mind coming to a different level with me?" Albin holds his hand out, palm up, but he's too far away for me to take it, so the gesture is weird.

"Sure," I say stiffly. "Let's go."

I catch Rhys's gaze one more time, briefly, and it seems like he's about to step forward, but he's smart enough to know that would guarantee both our deaths.

Albin passes me and steps out into the hallway.

My team is clearly unnerved.

"Good luck," P-230 says.

I nod my thanks, then follow Albin out the door.

He's waiting near the railing with that same big and beautiful smile.

"Hey, just relax," he says. "No one's in trouble." When he

talks, I can hear a bit of phlegm rattling in his lungs. *If he's sick, maybe he's weak.*

"I'm relaxed, just not feeling well," I say.

"Have you seen a doctor?" He sniffs.

I don't want to see a doctor. I just shrug and hope he drops it. We enter the elevator, and in the enclosed space I can smell him. He smells like cinnamon. Not like cinnamon scent, but actual cinnamon from a jar, slightly bitter.

He faces straight ahead, waiting patiently, until the car stops on level three. I follow him out, then halfway around the perimeter to a door that doesn't have a dorm label on it. Or any label. He pushes the door open and steps aside. "After you."

It's completely dark in the room, and every instinct says not to go in, but I can't just stand here. I step through the doorway, listening hard for the presence of others, but it feels empty. There's a slight plastic scent in the air.

Albin closes the door behind us and flicks on the light. I gasp at what I see. The room only holds a chair covered in thick chains. Adrenaline hits my bloodstream like a bomb. I whirl, but Albin backhands me across the face. It's like getting hit with a shovel. My head cracks into the wall and I slide down to the floor.

My vision is blurred on the right side from his slap, but he isn't taking advantage of my weakened state; he's just standing in front of the exit with his arms folded, a neutral look on his face.

"Sorry about that," he says. "Have a seat? I won't tie you up."

I get back on my feet and almost fall down. My head is throbbing, and I feel like my left side is heavier, like I'm going to tilt that way and crash into the wall again. *You should've stayed with Peter. No. You should've taken him and Rhys and just left this place behind.*

"Take a second. And then please sit down." He still hasn't moved and his eyes have never left me.

The heat from his blow has cooled to dull pain radiating down my face. I work my jaw around to make sure it's not broken. Then I sit down, mentally preparing myself to spring out of the chair if he takes a step closer. He doesn't.

"Are you a Rose?" I say, trying hard not to wince. My cheek is already swelling, making it painful to talk.

"No. My role is slightly different." He sniffles.

"Different how?"

"I can't tell you that, but I promise you'll know soon."

I imagine Rhys up in his dorm, and Peter in his. *Get out of the Verge,* I think. *Just go.*

"I know who you are, Miranda," Albin says. He snorts back snot and then spits it in the corner. The ball of phlegm is bloody.

"Are you sick?" I say. "What's wrong with you?" I make my tone prodding, trying to get a rise out of him.

"I know who you are," he says again.

"Care to share? I've been trying to figure it out for a while."

He laughs through his nose and somehow makes it sound delicate. "Humor. Very good. A fine reaction to danger. It's a mechanism to deal with fear. Some people, specifically people who aren't like us, usually choose panic. They shake. But you and fear are old friends, aren't you?"

I'm not sure what response he's looking for. Whatever it is, I want to give him the exact opposite. So I try one.

"That's interesting," I say.

"Mmm," he replies. "The director is excited that you're here, actually."

My blood runs cold. How did she find out? A moment passes where I consider opening my comm so I can at least warn Rhys to get out. But Albin only took *me* when he could have easily taken us both, so maybe his cover is still intact.

Albin smiles. "Yes, she knows you're here."

"I don't really give a shit." But after a moment I can't help myself. "Why is she excited?"

"That is my question to you. It appears I am uninformed about something. The director has a special interest in you, but no one can seem to tell me why. You aren't even a rumor among the ranks right now—everyone still thinks you're dead. Why is that?"

"No clue."

He doesn't say anything. I can tell he wants to sniffle again—his nose twitches, the nostrils inflamed—but he doesn't.

"You're sick," I say again, thinking hard, trying to buy myself some time.

"Do you know why I'm sick, Miranda?" The coolness in his voice is melting. I can tell I'm annoying him. Good.

"You don't get enough vitamin C?"

Albin lunges forward, stopping an inch from my face with both hands on the armrests, hovering over me. I keep staring right back into his eyes. I'm used to people trying to make me feel afraid.

"My sickness is why we're here." Fever radiates from his skin. I smell cinnamon again.

I wait, choosing not to speak.

He stands up straight, but keeps looking down at me. Something changes in his face. "I want you to understand something. True Earth is not evil. They are merely defending themselves. From you." *They,* he said. Not *we.* But the way he says it—it sounds canned. Like he's saying it for someone else's benefit. Someone watching us, perhaps?

Suddenly it hits me. *Defending themselves.* Albin hasn't been fully briefed. He doesn't know we're actually the past of True Earth, or True Earth is our future, however you want to put it. He still thinks True Earth is here to destroy us (or at least destroy us more than they're currently planning to).

I decide not to let on what I know, for now.

He snorts again, then drags his scaled forearm under his nose. "And I'm sick because of this *planet*. A planet full of people who willingly destroy themselves. How many people— actual *citizens* of this world—would end it all if they could? If they could press a button and erase everything? A hundred? A thousand? Millions, maybe. What do you think?"

"I think you should tell me exactly what you want from me and stop trying to rationalize mass murder." This isn't an interrogation. He's not asking me real questions. So what does he want?

Albin spits another glob of bloody phlegm on the floor. He closes his eyes. His eyelids flutter for a second, and then he fixes his stare on me once again. I have no idea what's going on.

He closes his eyes again, and I decide to stop waiting around. I explode out of the chair, whip open the door, and then vault over the railing. I was on level three, so it hurts when my feet smack the ground. Sharp pain travels from my feet up through my hips. I tuck myself into a forward roll and come up by a group of startled Roses. I shove through them and keep running. I don't want to leave Rhys or Peter behind, but our chances are better if we slip out separately.

No one shouts, no one follows. Outside it's as cold as ever, and the snow is blowing sideways. There's a Thorn twenty feet from the Verge, its driver's side door open. Too good to be true, but I'm not about to question it. My body is pure action, but my mind keeps drifting to random memories, the kind of stuff you recall without trying to. I see Peter's face, taste his mouth. I see the blood on Noah's face. I remember his arms around me, real only in my mind, right before we both died.

Noah may not be in my head anymore, but I know what he'd say. *Don't be afraid. And don't you dare give up.*

I'm not going to.

Then I'm inside the Thorn, tearing away from the Verge. The tires bite hard into the frozen ground. I run over a small tree like it's a toothpick. It's still all clear behind me, no pursuit. But I keep checking, because that can't be right—Albin should've sounded the alarm by now.

I drive west toward the apartment. Ten seconds after I leave the park, I pull over and ditch the Thorn. They'll be tracking it, no doubt. I get out, breathless from the adrenaline, and sprint the rest of the way, weaving up and down the streets, ignoring the citizens as they stare at me. My breath billows out in enormous clouds, the cold air stinging my throat.

I go in through the parking garage, stepping over the chunks of concrete I made with my RAW, then take the elevator up. The warm air is a shock, almost painful on my skin. I hunch over, hands on my knees, and just breathe while the car rises. By the time it gets to the top, I've almost caught my breath. Noble will know what the best plan is to get Rhys and Peter out. He'll know how to proceed. I'm almost smiling. I can't believe I made it out of there that easily. Some security force they've got there.

I fling the door open to our apartment and call out, "Noble! Sophia! Where are you?"

No response. I check each room. "Noble?"

R-34 and M-96 are gone too.

"Guys..." I say, even though I know I'm alone. I feel sick. I close my eyes.

When I open them, I'm back in the room with Albin, who is laughing his ass off.

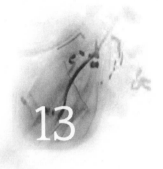

13

Albin doesn't stop laughing for a good twenty seconds. I almost think he's faking it.

I'm still in the chair. The chains are around me now, pinning me in place, cutting off circulation to my hands. I'm too confused to even be upset, like I'm waiting numbly for someone to explain the joke. I look down at my hands and open and close them, then squeeze, feeling the pressure in my palms. Albin laughs until he coughs and has to spit more phlegm.

"Too easy, too easy," he says.

I blink rapidly, then squeeze my eyes shut hard enough to make it hurt. When I open them, I'm still in the room. But how? It's impossible. I can remember the prickly warmth of the elevator, the way my lungs and throat burned from the cold air outside. It was real. And yet I'm here. Did they somehow incapacitate me in the apartment, then bring me back?

"You still don't get it," Albin says. He's calm again. "Hey, look, a cat!" He snaps his fingers. In the corner of the room there now sits a black cat. It stares at me, then begins to clean itself, licking a paw, then dragging it over its face. "Look," Albin says, "now it's gone." He snaps his fingers again, and the cat disappears.

I finally understand.

"You asked me if I was a Rose. I'm not a Rose, and I don't make people afraid. I make them see things. Anything I want. I made you see freedom. And where did you go? You went home."

He coughs again, and blood flecks his lips. "I stood beside you in your mind, on your journey through the snow." He wipes the blood away and leaves behind a smile. "Now I know where you live."

He says other things after that, but I can't hear him over the roaring in my ears. I've led the enemy to Sophia and Noble. *You didn't know,* I would like to tell myself, but I *should* have known. It was too easy. The Thorn was waiting for me right outside the door, and no one chased me. I should have known.

"Don't blame yourself," he says. "Actually, do. Your friends are going to die. But you're familiar with that, aren't you?"

The roaring in my ears filters into a frequency I can

understand, a signal I'm familiar with. Anger. "I'm going to kill you," I say.

"Call for your boyfriend," he says. "I know your Peter is here. I'm going to deal with him next. I'm going to make him see lots of things, I think. I'm going to make him see *you*, even after you're dead. And then when he thinks..."

He trails off as the door opens.

The director walks into the room.

She stands in the doorway for several seconds. Golden-haired, golden-scaled, she looks nothing like me, even though we have the same face. She is ancient in a way I can't explain. Sort of like how a vampire is old but looks young. She stares at me. Last time we came in contact, not counting our near miss on the street a few hours ago, she was trying to get her Torch back and I was planning to use it to destroy her army of eyeless. Which I did.

Yet here we are.

"Thank you, Albin," the director says, without looking away from me.

"I live to serve," Albin says, almost sarcastically but not quite. He leans in and whispers something in the director's ear.

"I bet you never thought you'd see me again," I say to her.

"Actually, I didn't know who you were until a few days ago."

Her words chill me, even though I'm not sure what she

means. Of course she knew who I was. I was the wrench in her works; I ruined her entire plan.

She steps closer and leans over me, close enough for me to smell her shampoo. And then her hands are undoing my chains. I think about biting her nose or ear off, but that's not going to get me out of here any faster. I try not to tremble. I try not to be afraid. Most of all, I try to gather some hope. But fail utterly. *We were just getting started*, I think. *I just got back. I just got to see Peter.* At least we had that final moment together. I picture his eyes, his lips, and the way his hands felt. I wear the memory like armor.

I don't want him to find me. I want him to run.

Another Miranda walks into the room. This one is different, though, and I recognize her instantly. She also has my face, but her hair is styled in a black pixie cut. This is Nina, *the* Nina, the original who loaned her identity to become a mole inside our team. I killed her in the Oval Office before she could send an army of monsters to eat our world from the inside out. I know this is the real her like I know anything.

"Remember when you killed me?" Nina says. She's smiling, giddy almost. "Revenge is sweet in any universe."

Universe. Does she know the truth about our worlds?

"Quiet, Nina," the director says.

"I do remember when I killed you," I say as the director

stands me up. I don't resist. What's the point? "Though you begged for your life." Nina did nothing of the sort, but I savor the reaction from her now. Her mouth actually falls open. She can't know what actually happened to the Nina I fought and killed—she wasn't there. "She must've been defective. I'm sure *you* would never beg."

The director guides me out of the room almost gently before Nina can respond.

"You have the same bad haircut, though," I say over my shoulder. "Interesting—" The director shoves me toward the railing and I grab on to it, but then her hands are on my legs and she's heaving me over the edge. From three floors up.

I flip once and land on my heels first, then butt, then back. Terrible pain flares horizontally through my shoulders and down my arms, and I can't breathe. *Bad pain,* I think. The kind of pain when you know you're really hurt; the kind that makes you afraid in a primal way.

Two feet thunk down next to me, and I follow them up to the director's face. She hovers over me, blotting out the light behind her.

"You've caused me a lot of trouble. So I have to punish you." She grabs my arm and pulls me up before I can catch my breath. A few Roses on the ground floor have stopped to watch. Above, Albin and Nina are leaning over the railing, staring down at us. Nina is grinning maniacally. The fire in my shoulders settles into my lower back, but I'm standing, so it's possible nothing is broken.

I finally get a decent breath, and the director actually supports me while I lean against her. She guides me out of the Verge, helping me as I limp along.

I cough and scratch out, "Where are we going?" then cough some more.

"I have to mold you now. You'll see."

I shove her off me, lose my balance, and almost fall to my knees. I recover, then stumble through the doors. The cold air hits me like a hammer.

"You can't run," she says calmly. "Not until I tell you something."

"Reveal your evil plan?" I say, coughing some more and tasting blood in my throat. My right eye is still blurry from Albin's strike.

You're in bad shape, North, I think in a calm way that scares me.

I'm too calm. Like I'm already accepting whatever comes next. Which is a cousin to giving up. "You should know that's always the villain's downfall," I continue.

"It's funny you use the word *villain,*" she says. "I wouldn't use that word."

I feel a deep, low thrum in my bones as the laser on top of the Verge fires into the sky again. The heat of it warms my neck. The laser drills a hole through the clouds, but I can't see what it strikes.

Then the director is on me, grabbing my arm and wrist for better leverage. Once again I let her.

"Tell me," I say. "Get it over with."

"First I have to show you something." We move through a line of leafless trees and enter a clearing, with the skyline visible in the gray distance. I begin to shiver, taking care not to look at the Time Warner Center, like that might give Noble and Sophia away. To the south, a phalanx of Axes hovers over the buildings. Silently I urge the director to keep moving farther from the Verge, away from Peter and Rhys.

I know your Peter is here, Albin said. Once Peter finds out what happened to me, he'll get out. He has to. Others are depending on him.

I can see where the Axes are moving now. Roses push through the trees. They circle around us in groups of five, but stay a respectful distance away. All the armor colors are represented. Albin is here too, lips stained with blood from his sickness. There have to be a hundred Roses out here now, all standing solid against the icy wind. I search for my Peter and Rhys among the faces, but they all look the same.

The director leans in close. "Olivia told me who you are. As she told me who I am. Olivia tampered with my memories, and it almost ruined everything. Actually, it did ruin everything.

But how can I hate the friend I've had for a thousand years?" She turns her face up to the sky. "Besides ... now we're here to fix it."

I'm shivering even harder. I'm sick of not understanding. I'm sick of all these layers.

"I forgive you for what you've done, Miranda, because you haven't learned yet. You have a long way to go. But it will happen. I know this because I exist." Her hot breath leaves my ear, and I almost miss it. She peers into my face, looking for some kind of understanding. I have nothing to show her.

"Just kill me," I say.

"You'll get smarter too," she says, squeezing my shoulder. "I'm not going to kill you. Because you're me."

That's when the Axes open fire. Each Ax gives off a tiny burst of light, and in the next second, the base of the Time Warner Center explodes.

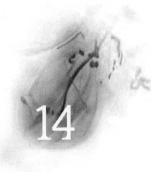

14

My scream is drowned out by the noise. First the deep bass of the explosion, and then the high-pitched screech and whine of the twisting iron inside the building. Both towers are leaning toward us, falling slowly, so slowly, and I only have time to think—*she said I am her*—before they pass some invisible line and come crashing down. The earth shakes, and a few Roses have to brace themselves against trees. The tops of the towers land hundreds of feet away, glass and debris flying toward us through the air like knives, and I want a few to pierce me so I won't have to feel what I'm feeling. The Black has nothing on the darkness inside me right now.

The wind fades away as the smashed towers settle into new

shapes. The air is filled with a choking gray dust. I can barely see ten feet in front of me.

The director is holding me up. "These are the moments that change you," she says. "Your only solace is that you will survive, Miranda. I'm not going to kill you. You are going to make the future. The Black leads to many eventualities, but sometimes a past and a future are linked. That just happens to be us."

The Roses are still watching us, waiting to see what happens next. Two buildings lie shattered next to them, and they seem bored with it all. I hear the director's words, and I choose to believe them for now, because denial isn't going to help me. I'm her, sure. Whatever. She's obviously got something wrong, because I can always kill myself. I can always choose.

As if she's reading my mind, the director peels the stamp off the base of my skull. If I die, and I'm somehow brought back again, that will be the last thing I remember.

That's when the darkness turns to fire; I decide to take control of my life. I swing my elbow up for her face, as fast as I can, with every ounce of strength I can muster.

She ducks underneath it.

"Fighting back is not in your best interest."

I barely hear her; I'm too busy trying to blast her head clean off with a punch. She steps aside easily, and I fall in the snow. The director grabs a hank of my hair and pulls me up to my knees, then kicks me in the face. My nose crunches, and blood flows out of my nostrils and coats my mouth and chin. It's so warm it actually feels good, my nose just this abstract throbbing thing that hasn't quite graduated to pain yet. I fall on my back, eyes blurry, and almost laugh. It's then that I know I'm losing it. I can tell in a kind of clinical, detached way. I try to remember a moment when I was happy. It had to be the dance, before Noah died. When a bright future didn't seem like that crazy of an idea. When I had my arms around Peter's neck, and we danced, and all of our problems were for tomorrow.

"There is more that has to happen today," the director says, staring down at me again. I can feel her, if not see through the tears. "You must be broken before you can rebuild, before you can be as strong as you'll need to be to lead your world into the future."

That's when an Olive and Noah march out of the Verge with Peter—my Peter. He's bound and gagged the way I found him in the basement of Key Tower, but this time his eyes are crazed and filled with rage. He's struggling, but the Roses hold him fast, pushing him toward us, lifting him when his feet stumble in the snow. I realize they're the Olive and Noah from our new "team"—O-9 and N-7. Peter is screaming behind his gag.

I lock eyes with him. He's shaking his head back and forth,

and I know if he could speak he'd be saying *I'm sorry* even though it isn't his fault. It's no one's fault.

"I know this hurts, Miranda," the director says. "But I promise time heals all wounds. I'm proof of that."

She pulls a sword off her back. I didn't even notice she was wearing one. In a flash I'm on my feet, even though my body is telling me to lie down. She flourishes the sword, and then lines it up horizontally with Peter's neck.

I charge ahead, knowing her blade will meet Peter's flesh before I'm halfway there, but I have to try anyway. I have to try.

There's a blur of motion from my right, a shape materializing from the dust, and then a Rhys is lunging forward with his own blade, meeting the director's in a burst of sparks. It's *my* Rhys. "Get out of here!" he screams to me. "Go!"

The director is laughing as her blade scrapes against his.

Rhys pushes hard against the director, and she stumbles back. Peter spins around, lifting his bound wrists as Rhys slices down and neatly severs his bindings.

In unison, a hundred Roses pull the swords off their backs.

The wind picks up, but it doesn't feel natural—it's too forceful, too sudden. Three seconds later, an Ax is hovering over the clearing, impossibly loud. The back hatch is open. The downward thrust flattens a pack of Roses ten feet away, pressing them hard into the snow and creating a whiteout effect. The air is nearly opaque with snow, steam, and dust.

Through the white, I see the blurred shape of Rhys engaged in a full-on duel with the director, swords swinging and crashing together, high low high. The snow at their feet is sprinkled with blood. Peter has my arm and he's pulling me backward toward the Ax, where a thick coil of rope dangles from the rear. He gets me in a bear hug.

"No! NO!" I'm screaming and struggling, trying and failing to pull his arm off my chest. I can't even jam my fingers under it. Peter keeps dragging me, slowly and relentlessly. Two Roses come at us, but gunshots from the Ax drop them. The people in the Ax are friends, but I don't care. Peter grabs the rope and suddenly we're ascending. Two hands pull us into the Ax—it's Sophia!

"I got you!" she says, and I feel a momentary burst of joy that she's still alive.

Down below, the director pushes Rhys back a few paces, then looks up. She screams something at me, but the roar is too loud, and I don't hear what it is.

I wipe the blood and tears off my face, then try again to get free. I stomp on Peter's foot, but that only makes him clench harder.

"Help Rhys!" Sophia cries out.

"We'll get him! We'll get him!" Peter says.

The Ax banks to the right, the rope dangling by Rhys. Two Roses lunge for it, but Rhys spins, severing the rope high above his head to keep them from grabbing it. He slashes both their throats with the same spin, scales from their armor flying with the blood.

In the next second the downward thrust from the Ax's vertical engines knocks Rhys over. He scrambles in the snow for his sword.

"Move away!" I scream to the pilot. The Ax slides sideways a little, just a few feet.

"Let out more rope!" Peter yells.

But it's too late. Rhys gets to his sword, but a Noah—it has to be N-7—steps on the center of his back, pulling his own sword off his back. Rhys tries to drag himself along, but N-7 has him pinned. He can't even roll out of it. The director holds up her hands, and she's screaming something at N-7, but no one can hear her over the roaring engines. N-7 isn't looking at her, or he would stop. He would stop, but he doesn't.

I'm screaming Rhys's name when N-7 raises his sword up, then plunges it straight down into the center of Rhys's back.

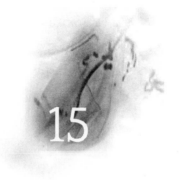

15

Things happen in the seconds after that, but I'm not completely aware of them. I know Sophia is screaming. I know I fight Peter off, or try to. I know I almost make it out the back hatch again, but this time Peter gets an arm around my neck. He's screaming something too. I stop fighting as the Ax ascends, and just watch, so I can remember.

The snow under Rhys is red on both sides. He isn't moving, and I know he'll never move again. The sword in his back leans slightly to the left. A dozen silver-suited Roses are pulling the RAWs off their backs, but the director gives a cutting hand signal, and they stop. She takes four steps and slashes out with her own sword, severing N-7's head from his neck. He stands upright for two full seconds as everyone around him backs away, exchanging terrified looks.

Now the director is saying something to Albin. He nods, turns his face toward us, and closes his eyes. In the next moment, I am struck completely blind. All I see is darkness. But my other senses are intact. I can hear the ship around me, feel the vibrations in the soles of my feet, and then my knees, when I fall to them. Peter drops with me, still holding me tight against his chest, his arm an iron bar across my body.

"Bank right! Bank right!" I hear someone yell from the front. It sounds like Noble, which makes the fist around my heart relax just slightly. Noble's alive too. Of course he is. Who else could rescue us, after all?

The Ax shifts violently to the right, throwing me and Peter and Sophia against the wall. I slip from Peter's grasp and fall on my stomach near the still-open hatch. The turbulent wind at the opening thrashes my face, and I relish the pain, the little ice particles that bite into my skin. I could pull myself another foot and fall through the opening and never have to deal with this shit again. I wouldn't have to lose anyone else. I wouldn't have to become the director. I still can't believe that's even a possibility—but why would she lie? For what purpose? Does it fit with what Olivia told me? I need to see what's on the disk. If events happening here have an effect on the future of True

Earth, then I still have a choice. Maybe I have an opportunity to change it all.

Besides, if I died now, the director still has my memory stamp. She could just bring me back.

The voices from the front of the Ax are panicked. I feel us slowing down. "I can't see a damn thing!" an unfamiliar voice shouts. A man, but not Noble.

An alarm starts blaring. I still can't see, but it sounds like we're flying down a street, tall buildings amplifying the engine noise on both sides.

"Brace for impact!" Sophia shouts. The metal under my left hand starts rising; the rear hatch is closing.

I press my face against the cold metal floor of the Ax. Peter pulls himself on top of me, covering my body with his. He presses his cheek against mine, so it's warm on the right side of my face, freezing on the left.

"I love you," Peter whispers in my ear. All I can do is nod, but he feels it with his face against mine.

In the next second, the Ax collides with something, and we fly straight up into the ceiling. The darkness continues, but in a different way.

I blink myself awake and find that I can see again. The first thing that settles on me, the first thing I *feel*, is disappointment, and that makes me ashamed. I wanted the darkness to last forever. There are too many things to think about right now—I can't even order them.

She said Olivia had tampered with her memories somehow. Does that mean she doesn't know what I'm going to do next? If I'm truly her, wouldn't she remember and be able to find us right away?

No, otherwise we would've never gotten away in the first place.

Unless she just knows we'll be captured later.

The uncertainty is a scream rising in my throat, one I have to choke down like poison. *Which is it?*

Someone else groans in the hatch, and I feel Peter's hand brush across my face. I can't see out of my right eye, and when I try to move, pain bursts down from the back of my skull into my nose and right shoulder. So I don't try to move. The Ax is upside-down, the back hatch wrenched open. Snow is blowing into the compartment. I hear the whistle-roar of a turbo diesel engine close by—Humvees.

I try to push myself up with my left hand, but it's useless. I can't feel it at all. I look at it. The scales have been stripped off the armor, and my last two fingers are swollen, making the material underneath the scales bulge.

Now that I can see my hand, it begins to hurt.

Badly.

Peter is seated across from me, holding his knee. Otherwise he looks all right. His eyes scan my body, looking for damage, wincing when they find it.

"You okay?" he says.

"No," I reply.

I turn my head to the left and see Noble standing over me, his hair and beard matted with blood. He's clearly dazed, eyes unfocused. Either a concussion, or Rhys's death.

"Miranda," he says. There are human shapes behind him, but I can't make them out. I reach up and touch my right eye to make sure it's still there; it is. Just swollen. "How did he die?"

"Cleanly." I say the lie through fat lips.

He nods, then helps Sophia to her feet. She's just coming to, and once again I'm filled with relief that they weren't in the Time Warner Center. I want to continue feeling good about it, but their survival isn't a victory. Everyone in the towers is still dead. All because I revealed the location.

Noble grabs Sophia and they embrace tightly. He strokes the back of her hair as she cries silently into his chest. "It's okay," he says, but it isn't, and it never will be.

The diesel engines are so close now. I hear heavy doors open and slam shut. I hear parts of heavy rifles clicking and clacking, boot steps muffled by the snow, orders being shouted back and forth. Through the gap in the hatch, I see a flash of urban camouflage, blue, gray, and white. There is no sense of urgency inside the Ax; we're just waiting. The people outside are not Roses, but that doesn't mean they're any less dangerous. There is nothing more dangerous than a human who is afraid.

Peter crawls over to me, grimacing against the pain. He sits down and loops his arm around my shoulder, then kisses me on the cheek, leaving a smear of blood. He's looking at me like he can't believe I'm here. He kisses me on the other cheek, and the forehead, and keeps looking at me. He shakes his head.

"You're alive," he says, and then presses his cheek to mine. The stubble on his chin pricks my skin, and it is a good feeling. "I can't do it again, Miranda. I won't watch you die. Say you won't."

"I think my hand is really hurt," I say tonelessly. Perhaps I'm in shock. "And I won't."

"These people will fix it," he says. "We're alive, that's all that matters."

Is it?

The soldiers outside get the back hatch the rest of the way open by connecting it to a Humvee and wrenching it down. Bright white light fills the Ax. My eyes adjust, and I see a dozen or so soldiers pointing their rifles in our direction. Peter positions himself in front of us, a shield.

The stranger in the front of the Ax unbuckles himself from the pilot's chair, falls hard in a clump, then staggers upright, pressing a palm to his temple. I focus hard with my good eye and can barely make out the details of his face. His identity is confirmed a moment later, when a soldier yells, "Holy shit! It's him!" and another yells, "That's the guy they're looking for!"

I turn toward the man again and see what Noah would look like if he'd lived long enough to become a middle-aged man.

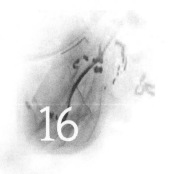

16

The soldiers rush inside and grab East first, shoving him to the floor/ceiling of the Ax and binding his hands behind his back with quick, precise movements. They load him into the nearest Humvee, which takes off two seconds later. I look through the open hatch at the sky, but there are no pursuing Axes, no Thorns in the street. Just swirling snow; it's begun to fall again, with enthusiasm.

Why aren't they coming after us?

Because the director could already know where we are.

But if she already knows everything, then why haven't we lost yet? How are we still alive? What am I supposed to do?

If I'm her in the future, then a thousand years or more have passed for her. Would she be remembering these events as they happen? Maybe not. It could be fuzzy, or things could've played out differently. They must have. It doesn't make sense otherwise.

I touch the pouch holding Olivia's disk. *Soon.*

More soldiers pour in. They grab Peter first and yank him upright. "We're on your side," Peter says calmly. "Who's in charge? I was on my way to meet with some soldiers when the attack—"

"Shut your mouth," the soldier handling him says.

Someone else barks, "If they do the fear thing, drop them. Got it?"

They think we're the enemy, which is understandable. We're a bunch of clones in a crashed enemy fighter. A soldier picks me up roughly, then eases his grip when he sees my face. That doesn't stop his partner from binding my wrists.

"I'm not the bad guy," I slur.

He doesn't know what to say to that, so he and his partner just march me out the back. I thought it was cold in the Ax, but I was wrong.

"What if they're being tracked?" a soldier says. I blink rapidly, trying to force my right eye open, but I can't even tell if the lid is moving.

"Scan 'em," another replies. I pick up my feet to walk, but my left knee is suddenly being unhelpful. The two soldiers are basically dragging me along.

We stop in front of a wiry soldier an inch shorter than I am. He's wearing a blue beret, which makes me want to laugh for some reason. He has a lantern jaw and a dusting of silver facial hair. His narrowed eyes scan me. The nameplate above his heart says R. KELLOGG.

"Why did you crash?" he says to me.

"Long story," I reply.

Another soldier approaches me with a handheld scanner. The long antenna makes scratchy noises as it passes over my body.

"Have you been briefed on Rhys Noble?" I turn my head toward the hatch. "The man right there? We're on your side."

He stares at me a beat longer. The soldier with the scanner stops on my forearm, where the display is. "There's something in her suit, right here."

"If the Roses were coming, they'd be here." I point at the sky back the way we came. There is grayish dust and black smoke above the buildings where the Time Warner Center fell. A few Axes are visible beyond that. "See? Talk to Peter. He's been working with you—*hello*—do you know *anything*?"

"Relax, Mir," Peter says. "We'll straighten it out once we're off the street."

Kellogg ignores me. "Cut her sleeve off. Cut the boy's off too."

"Uh, that's not going to work."

A soldier tries with his knife anyway. It goes about as well as you'd expect. He barely succeeds in scratching the scales.

"Should we strip them?" the soldier with the knife asks. They're all wearing camo helmets with snow goggles, so I can't tell them apart.

"Try it and see what happens," Peter says behind me.

"Please," Noble says, staggering up beside us. He and Sophia are similarly bound. "Where is General Davis? He'll know who we are."

"General Davis is dead," Kellogg says. Then back to his colleague, "We just go the long way. They'll lose their signal underground. I want to study the suits."

"That's a bad idea," I say. "The tunnels are full of spiders made out of human arms." I feel drunk. Shocked. I am in shock, I think.

Kellogg squints at me curiously. "I'm aware. We've secured a section of tunnel." He takes a deep breath and then bellows, "Let's move!"

Some of the soldiers pile into the Humvees and leave, while a few form a perimeter around us and march us down the nearest subway steps. The subway platform is warmer than the street above, but just barely. Hopping the turnstile is more painful than I expected. The platform is deserted, but the lights are still on. We hop down onto the tracks. It's a difficult jump to make while bound, and I fall on one knee, my bad knee. Peter falls hard on his shoulder, splashing into a puddle between the tracks.

The soldiers get us upright again, not necessarily rough, but not treating us gently, either.

"Easy," Kellogg says to them. "Respect."

We start our march down the tunnel. I keep my good eye open, scanning for spiders. I keep jumping at shadows, but there's nothing there. No clawed hands to grab my ankles and pull me into darkness.

Next to me, Sophia trips on a tie and splashes down in another puddle.

"Help her, dammit!" Noble says when the soldiers are slow to move. They get her back to her feet. She looks as miserable as I feel, her mouth loose in a grimace, as if she's about to scream.

We march for what seems like miles. Flashlights illuminate the way ahead, but only for so many feet. Two soldiers eventually have to support Peter on either side, his knee is so bad. My nose throbs, and the pain in my left hand grows hotter. I'm scared to take the glove off and see what it looks like.

"Rhys knew what he was doing," Peter whispers. His voice is nearly swallowed by the echoing footsteps in the tunnel walls.

"So what?" I say.

He doesn't say anything after that.

"I'm sorry," I say a few minutes later.

Eventually there is literal light at the end of the tunnel, flickering red, and soon after I can see that the glow comes from burning flares on the ground. There are more soldiers guarding the next subway platform, some kneeling around the rails, guns pointed at us.

"Sound off," one soldier calls.

"It's Kellogg," Kellogg replies.

The soldiers hold their positions until we get closer. They tense up when they see Peter and me.

"Jesus," a young guy with a beard says. "You brought them *here*?"

A soldier named Q. Tavaras says, "We heard they had the fugitive with them. Is it true?"

"It is," Kellogg says. "Give these two medical attention"—he points at Peter and me—"and have the man and other girl checked out. I want a full guard on them at all times." He jumps onto the platform, then turns around and looks down on us. "I'm going to have my men remove your restraints. Is that going to be a problem?"

"No, sir."

His look softens. "I hope what you've been saying is true. We need an ally."

I nod. "So do we."

He jogs away from the group, down a set of stairs, as the

soldiers remove our restraints. This is one of the underground entrances to Penn Station, I discover. Getting up onto the platform is even more painful than getting down; I can only use one hand, and the effort makes my nose feel like it's about to burst open. I must be really out of it, because I don't notice the pile of spider corpses until I'm standing next to it. The tangled heap of black arms is slashed with blood in places, the clawed hands upturned and open.

The soldiers march us down the same stairs, up a ramp, and then we're in a long and tall tunnel with a dozen restaurants stretching away from us on the left. There is trash all over the floor, but a few soldiers are cleaning it up with huge push brooms, shoving everything into neat piles. The metal gates on all the shops are up, but most of the lights are out. The soldiers pause in their cleanup to watch us with suspicious eyes. *I'm on your side,* I'd say, if I knew they'd believe me.

We go up a final set of stairs, past more armed soldiers, and step onto the main floor of Penn, the one with the giant sign in the middle that would normally be showing what tracks the trains would be departing from. Right now it's blank. Refugees are spread out all over—there is nothing else to call them. Some of them have suitcases. They're just sitting around, waiting. Seeing them makes me angry for some reason. I don't know if I'm mad they're just sitting there, waiting for someone to save them, or if I'm just mad about everything. I want answers, of course, but they're not going to let me talk to East, even if I ask nicely.

The soldiers guide us along, shielding us from view. A refugee sees us anyway and cries out like someone stabbed him or something. A few other people look, but by then we're hustling past them, around a corner and off the main floor.

My injured hand brushes my thigh, and the pain flares up like a stoked log. I can't even imagine what it looks like. The fingers could be severed inside the glove for all I know, and for all I feel. I suspect I won't have to imagine much longer.

We follow the path into another open area, where gurneys have been set up in rows, along with trays of instruments and random medical monitors here and there. It's a thrown-together medical station. Luckily, there's only one man being treated for a long cut on his forearm. But I notice a few of the other beds are stained with patches of blood from previous patients. I can't imagine the number of injuries sustained in the panic during and after the initial assault.

The soldier who seems to be in charge—a sergeant, judging by the patch on his sleeve—raises a hand at two women in scrubs. "Move these two into the Taco Bell. I want them out of sight."

The two women recoil at first and actually stop their approach.

"It's fine," the sergeant says.

They share a look; it's clear they've been working together for a while. They could be sisters. Both of them have dyed-red hair.

They push some gurneys into the Taco Bell, which is hollowed out, the chairs and tables ripped from the floor, leaving gaping holes in the tile. I get that Manhattan doesn't have a military base, but this is the best they could come up with? Penn Station has more entrances and exits than I can count. I can only hope they're waiting for reinforcements to make their way through the city ... otherwise it feels like they're just waiting for True Earth to find them, or for the cold to kill them.

Peter and I stand there uselessly, trying to stay upright. The women get the lights turned on, then beckon for us to lie down on the beds. I drop my guard simply because I can't keep it up any longer.

The woman won't look at my eyes. She has a HI MY NAME IS sticker on her shirt, which says LAURIE.

"Hi, Laurie," I say.

She jumps and drops her clipboard like it's hot. Then she closes her eyes and takes a breath.

"I'm sorry about what's happening," I offer. "I promise you I had nothing to do with it."

A lie if the director is telling the truth about who I am.

Laurie nods. "Your hand is injured."

Thinking about it brings a fresh burst of pain.

152

"Your tools won't cut through the armor," I say.

She nods, chewing her lower lip, hovering over me, her fear temporarily forgotten in the face of a new problem.

"Can you shrug out of it?" she asks.

I look at my hand again. The armor is so swollen I think I'd pass out before I could peel it over the skin.

"The seam at the wrist," Peter says a few feet away. His eyelids are heavy; the nurse has already medicated him. His bad knee is stretched out on the table, the other hugged to his chest with both hands.

To compensate for my swelling hand, the armor at the seam has already started to separate. Smart, otherwise I'd be in even bigger trouble.

I pull at the seam to get it started. A few of the scales snap apart like teeth on a zipper, and then a thick stream of blood pours out from the bottom and onto Laurie's shoes.

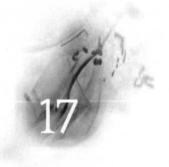

17

I'm going to lose my hand. The nurse doesn't have to say anything; I can tell by her face. The first thing she does is run for a doctor. Peter is trying to get off his gurney to help me, but he's too far gone, and his nurse doesn't have much trouble keeping him on his back. She gives him another syringe full of something, and he sinks into the pillow, eyes shut. Good. I don't want him to see this.

Me? I'm crying. I'm not sure if it's from the pain or from the knowledge that something bad is going to happen to me—something that will make it harder to fight. I remember the director again. She has both hands. So I should have both hands too, right? Or maybe one is bionic, who knows.

Or maybe she was lying. I'm still not convinced.

I won't know until I see Olivia's memories.

Blood is still pouring out of my glove. It started as a river as thick as my wrist, but has tapered to a pencil-thin stream. I can't feel my ring and little fingers. Come to think of it, I can't feel my face. *Take heart,* I think. *You are still alive, and the fight is not over.* The thought is surprisingly articulate, given the general fuzziness in my brain. Noah and Rhys and Olive are not alive, but I know what they'd do if they were—they'd keep fighting. So I will in their place.

God, I miss them.

The doctor comes over and begins working on my glove. He actually gasps when it comes off. I still don't look at my hand. But I feel the cool air on it, so that's good.

"Give her something, Laurie. Jesus."

Laurie gives me something. A needle gently inserted into my neck, since my arms are still armored. Something to make me sleep. I am grateful.

I wake up in a KFC. We're doing the fast food medical tour, I guess.

Kellogg stands next to my bed, and there are two armed soldiers in the corner. His eyes flick to my left hand, so I follow his gaze and find my hand wrapped in approximately four hundred pounds of gauze. It looks like a freaking club. But I feel great. It feels like my blood has been swapped out with . . .

something incredible, I don't know. I am a blanket. I could lie here forever, if I didn't have things to do. I'm still wearing my red armor, but it ends just above my left elbow now. I have no idea how they got through it.

My nose is covered in a bandage, and it feels worse and better at the same time, which I assume means someone set it for me.

"I've been briefed on the alliance Noble had with General Davis," Kellogg begins without preamble. "Davis was in charge, but now I am. Apparently not many people knew that Noble and his team have been working with us."

"Good," I begin.

"*But...* I want to know why you look exactly like the people we're fighting. Noble gave me a story, but I want to hear it from you now."

I don't have the energy to be angry at his demands. It's either the drugs or that I understand where he's coming from. Probably both. I just now realize that I still can't see out of my right eye.

"No offense, but I don't give a damn about what you want to know. I just saw my friend die." My voice is so nasal I barely recognize it. I'm breathing out of my mouth, since my nose feels like it's plugged with concrete.

"We've all seen friends die," he says flatly.

"Where is Peter? How did you and your men get on the island?"

He pauses, clearly debating whether to answer. "My men and I are stationed here permanently. There is always a military presence in Manhattan, in case it becomes separated from the outside world. When the attack happened, we were activated. It is my understanding that the defense of the city was still being planned when the attack came. That's why we haven't organized a full retaliation. Communications with the mainland—and my superiors—seem to be disrupted for now."

"I want to see my team."

"They're resting in different rooms. Safe and sound."

I look away as a wave of nausea passes over me, leaving me light-headed.

"If you say we're on the same side, you'll want to help us understand. . . ." Kellogg leaves the idea hanging. "Davis did not share his plans with me before he was killed. I didn't have the clearance. Technically, I still don't."

"Let me talk to the prisoner. Then we'll discuss understanding."

After a moment, he nods. "You'll be under surveillance."

"Of course. What does my hand look like?"

"Not good," he says. "Two of the—"

A burst of machine gun fire cuts him off. It came from down the hallway, loud enough to make me jump.

"Stay here," he says, pulling his sidearm off his thigh and

sidestepping out of the KFC. The two soldiers follow Kellogg, leaving me alone. People are screaming down the hallway.

A man is yelling, "SPIDERS! SPIDERS!" at the top of his lungs.

The adrenaline spike quickens my heart, which quickens the throb in my wounds. There is a knife in my skull I'd like to remove. I give the restaurant a quick once-over, but there are no weapons, and nothing I could turn into one easily. I remember when I first saw the spiders in the tunnels. How there was darkness, and then they were visible all at once.

I get off the bed and almost fall to my knees. The velvety feeling in my body has evaporated; instead, hot lead has settled into my hand, which I'm hoping I never have to look at. Kellogg said *Two of the*. Two of the what? Fingers? Are broken, missing, destroyed?

I take a step forward and almost rip an IV out of my arm. I follow the line up to a bag next to my bed, then grab it off the hook and hold it in my good hand.

I stagger out of the restaurant as more machine gun fire boxes my ears. Soon soldiers are yelling "Clear!" back and forth to one another. Threat eliminated, for now. I stand in the big open space until Kellogg jogs back to me. I just don't have the energy to wander off on my own.

He takes my arm and guides me toward a hallway. "Don't

move again unless someone tells you to. You need an escort at all times."

"I wasn't handcuffed."

"It doesn't matter."

"How many spiders were there?" I pull the catheter out of my arm and set the IV bag on a nearby gurney. Someone else will make better use of it.

"Three," he says. "They push at us every few hours, like they're testing our strength."

"So True Earth knows your location. Which means eventually they will come for you." We pass more refugees, who visibly shrink away from us, or me. Their fear brings me a different kind of pain.

"I know they'll come for us. Maybe they're waiting for the best opportunity to minimize casualties on their side, so we'll just keep that opportunity out of reach."

"What's your *plan*?"

"Right now we simply don't have the numbers, or the weapons, to stage an attack."

"Well, by all means, keep wasting time, then," I say. Though honestly I'm not sure what they should do, either.

Kellogg stops outside the men's bathroom. "East's in here."

"Seriously?"

He nods. "You have two minutes."

I hobble into the bathroom, round a corner, and meet an armed guard who doesn't make eye contact or speak to me. Twenty feet behind him is East. The creator is on his knees between the stalls and the urinals. He's wrapped in chains, and his wrists are secured to the floor on either side, connected to spikes driven right into the tile. He lifts his head slowly. His hair is longer than Noah kept his, and he's wearing round eyeglasses. He looks like a kindly man who isn't quite old yet, but is working on it.

"It's good to meet you, Miranda," he says to me.

I just stare at him.

"I assume you've been given a short amount of time to speak to me, in return for something else."

I nod, walking toward him.

"That's very good. What's your first question?"

"How did Noble find you?"

He lifts one eyebrow. "That's your first question?"

"I want to know it's not a trap."

He nods thoughtfully. "Not bad. Noble was monitoring a radio frequency we used to use back in the day, as I hoped he would. I sent coordinates over it in Morse code when I could. Doing so I took the chance that the other creators would be able to find me, but I've since learned that we're the only two left, thank the Lord."

"Yeah, I wasn't a fan of them overall."

"Neither was I," he says. "I only wish I'd had the courage to approach Noble before he left, to let him know how I felt. I would've joined him. The creators were always fighting amongst themselves. True Earth took a hands-off approach. We only knew about them in a very ancillary way, and it was mostly Mrs. North, as you called her, who had the connection. The rest of us were just following orders, doing what we had been raised to believe was our duty." He gazes at the ceiling, and gives a thoughtful smile. "God rest her miserable, wretched soul."

He doesn't say anything else, so I ask, "What is the Key?"

His eyes flick down momentarily. "I am the Key. If I travel through the Black, I can choose to enter a room that exists outside of space and time. From that room, one can end any of the universes. Or a war." Just like Olivia said—*possess the Key, control the Black.* She didn't say anything about East himself being the Key, though.

"But you know True Earth is part of this time line, right? You know we're linked?"

He nods. "That doesn't mean they aren't a threat to us now. What is time to immortal beings?"

"I don't know what that means."

The skin around his eye twitches, like a tic. "Mmm. There is much you don't seem to know at this point. True Earth is here to re-create a nuclear war they accidentally stopped, but one that was entirely necessary for the world to become what they perceive as 'perfect.' Do you understand?"

Nuclear war? "How did they stop it?"

"Since you stopped the eyeless, the nuclear war that was in your future will never come to pass the way it would have if True Earth hadn't interfered in the first place. Instead the world will unite and put aside its differences. You were only a few years away from complete annihilation, but now we're all brothers with a common enemy. Don't you see?"

"So because I stopped the eyeless, I stopped the coming world war, which alters the future."

He nods. "Exactly. If they had never brought the eyeless in the first place, things would've gone as planned . . . but I guess someone wasn't *in the know*, as they say."

"Why don't you want them to re-create the effect of war?"

He looks at me as though the answer is completely obvious, and maybe it is, but I don't know where his allegiances lie. "We should let them kill billions now in an effort to preserve their one idea of the future? To preserve their perfect True Earth? No, I will not go along with that willingly."

"How did you feel about it before? Back when True Earth didn't know we were part of the same universe? When they just wanted to wipe us out like *animals*?" My voice catches and I force myself to lower it. That minor exertion has me feeling dizzy. I blink.

"How did I feel? I felt appalled. That's why I left the creators, not too long after Noble, actually. I didn't like what we were doing. I wanted to do other things."

East doesn't sound very much like Noah. His voice is a little deeper, and the words are different. I can still hear the same attitude beneath them, though.

"Am I the director?" I whisper, hopefully too quiet for any ears other than East's to hear. East seems to know a lot, and this might be my only chance to get an outside opinion. Surely if Noble knew, he would've told me by now.

East recoils, almost dramatically. The chains scrape on the floor. "Why would you say that? Who told you that?"

"She did. She said she had to mold me. She said she didn't even know who I was until a few days ago, she—"

"Stop," he says sharply, before I can say more. "We're being watched." His eyes go to the ceiling in the corner, where a hastily installed camera is nestled.

He lets his gaze fall to the tiled floor. He starts shaking his head back and forth, lips moving in silence.

"What is it? Tell me," I say.

"You need to free me," he says, raising his eyes to mine. The desperation in them chills me to my core. "Or everything is lost."

18

I don't have the option, because Kellogg is stalking toward me from the left. "Time's up," he says, grabbing my arm. A fresh lance of pain rolls from my thumb to my shoulder.

"Easy," I say, shrugging away from him. "I am not your prisoner."

His little blue beret is askew. He's within arm's length. I could grab his Adam's apple and crush it; I think I'm fast enough for that, even with the wounds and drugs.

But he nods, which is a step in the right direction.

"I have more questions for him," I say.

"You'll get to speak later."

Kellogg pulls me away, and I let him. When I look back a

final time, East is staring at the floor again, his lips moving in silence. He was supposed to be able to help us.

"Where are you taking me?" I ask Kellogg.

"You wanted to see your team, right?"

Kellogg takes me into a Hudson News and through the back room (but not before I grab a bottle of Advil off the medicine rack), into the corridors that run behind the stores for garbage disposal. We have to step over full trash bags, which feels like hurdling a car. I know I shouldn't be up and walking around, but I don't care. I pop four Advil and dry-swallow them.

We enter a garage filled with overflowing trash bins. The garage doors are shut, and even from this distance I can see the fresh, sloppy welds along the edges. No exit that way. But they're fooling themselves if they think a couple welds are going to keep True Earth out when they decide to ruin our little party.

Filling the garage are two M1 Abrams tanks, the main tank used by the US military since 1980. I suppose the soldiers won't really need to open the doors for the tanks to roll out when it comes down to it.

Noble is standing in the middle of the room, between the two tanks, with three soldiers and Peter. Sophia is nowhere to be seen. The soldiers are standing with their rifles held tightly to their chests. They keep a safe distance, which shows how much they trust us at this point.

Peter's face falls when he sees mine; I must really look damaged. Noble winces. Peter takes a step toward me and then wobbles midstride. Noble has to sling an arm around him to hold him up. Peter grits his teeth.

"I want answers, and I want them quickly," Kellogg says.

"You can't destroy the Verge," Noble says to him.

I wasn't aware they were planning on attacking it.

"Why not?" Kellogg replies.

"Because there is an entrance to the Black inside it. It's the only one nearby. If you destroy the Verge, the wreckage will cover it and we'll never get inside."

"Then tell me how to beat these people, Mr. Noble," Kellogg says.

"First, I need to know what East has done with the Key."

"He says *he* is the Key," I say.

Noble tilts his head sideways. "I see."

Peter steps toward me, and I take some of his weight. I can feel his leg trembling with the strain; he shouldn't be out of bed. If we're going to keep fighting, that knee has to heal.

I'm eager to tell Noble and Peter what else East told me, but I still don't trust Kellogg and his men completely.

"Give us some time alone," I say to Kellogg. "When we figure things out, we'll let you know."

Kellogg makes a show of considering it. He doesn't like it, but what else is he going to do? "Fine, but you don't have long. These people have some of my men in an internment camp. In the freezing cold. I'm going to get them back."

I only nod.

"And I'm still waiting for an answer about why you look like the people out there."

"I understand," I say. But I have no idea how to really explain that to him.

Kellogg leads us back to the KFC, where I lie down again. He leaves right away, without a word. A nurse rolls Peter's bed inside for him to lie on, and Noble sits down in one of the booths.

"Where is Sophia?" I say, looking at the faces outside in the open area.

"Getting some rations for us to share," Noble replies. "She's remarkably uninjured, save for some crushed cartilage in her ear."

Peter breathes a heavy sigh of relief. "That's fantastic. Seriously."

"Yes, it is," I say, wondering how she's doing on the inside. Rhys never got to tell her how he felt ... and she never got to hear it. "Are we going to talk about Rhys?"

Noble shakes his head slowly, not looking at anything. I know what Rhys meant to him. In the beginning, Noble raised him as a son.

"I think we should."

"It's not going to help us win," he says, a little harshly.

"You don't care enough to talk about it? Why are you here, then?" I regret the questions as they come out of my mouth. It's lashing out for no good reason.

Noble stares me right in the face now. "I am offended by that question."

"Miranda," Peter says. "People mourn in different ways."

And suddenly I'm ashamed.

Noble's eyes are red, and his lower lip is trembling, or maybe that's just my monovision. "I am trying to make things right. I am fighting back against what I am. Don't ever imply I don't care again, Miranda. I will mourn later, when the rest of my family is safe."

His words are like a dagger to my heart. I don't know why I said what I did. Being angry and upset and confused isn't an excuse.

"I'm sorry. I didn't mean it," I say.

"I understand," Noble says. Of course he does.

"I'd like to fight back against what I am too," I say. "The director said I'm her. Or that I will become her in the future." The words come out in a rush. Now my friends know, and they'll help me figure it out no matter what.

Peter shakes his head, brow furrowed. "That's not true. It's more mind games. You would never be like her."

"That's not all," I say. "Both she *and* Olivia—the *Original* Olivia—say True Earth isn't really a different universe at all, but just a future of this one."

Noble has no reaction. None.

"Is that true, Noble?" I press.

Finally he says, "You know, I really can't say."

I let my head fall onto the pillow. The throb in my face has changed into the sting of a thousand biting ants. But I get right back up again when I really think about his reaction. "You knew it was a possibility but didn't tell us? Why?"

He just shakes his head slowly. "Miranda, I did not think it was a possibility. I don't know much about the Black, or True Earth. Only what Olivia told me. And she didn't tell me that."

Time passes and no one says a word. If Rhys were here, maybe he'd say something to fill the silence. A joke that isn't really a joke. I took him for granted, that's for sure. I had no idea how much I would miss him. He never talked about it, not ever, but I know what haunted him. Rhys killed his entire team to save them from the creators. And it changed him forever. *But now you're free.*

Olive, Noah, Rhys . . . all gone. How much longer can we last?

"There is no such thing as destiny, Miranda. You should know that." Noble's voice startles me, sets my heart pounding.

"Explain."

He scratches at his beard. His lower eyelids are red-rimmed and sagging. "Well, True Earth might be one future, but it doesn't have to be the only future. It is just one possibility. By changing things here, we're moving down a new course. Theoretically."

"Right," Peter says. "If the director says you're supposed to become her, how can that be true if you don't want it to be? Just *don't become her.*"

"I don't *plan to,*" I say.

Noble raises both hands, palms out. "Stop it. Their future is not relevant. I repeat—*not relevant.* Because what we care about are the people living *right now*, isn't that so? We're not going to engineer some event they think needs to happen just to preserve what they know as the future—there are too many variables involved with that anyway. They've tinkered with their past and now they're paying the price." His eyes flit between us, making sure we're listening very closely, which we are. He takes a shuddering breath. "But we still have to win. That hasn't changed. You think Rhys would just surrender?"

"No one is talking about surrender," I say calmly.

After a moment, he nods, eyes on the floor. Finally he looks at me with semiclear eyes. "Yes, well, you can never be too sure. It doesn't matter what time lines the other universes belong to, or which ones are linked, or if they're connected to our world. What matters is *this* world. Let's keep that in mind going forward. Let's stay the course. Let's ignore everything else." His voice wavers on the last sentence and almost breaks on *else*.

Another length of silence, the weight of which I can feel in my blood. Helplessness is still a specter looming outside our doorway.

"For now, you two need to rest," Noble says. "You have injuries."

That's when Sophia returns with an armload of military MREs—Meals Ready-to-Eat. Not delicious, but nutritious. She doesn't make eye contact with anyone, just wordlessly hands them out. She also has a few pieces of dried-out pizza, which she holds up in offer.

"Sophia..." I say.

"Don't," she says. "I don't want to hear anything from anyone right now." Her lower lip quivers. "Not a word."

I nod. Through a throbbing jaw, I eat some food that tastes like nothing. And I prepare for the moment when I can finally see Olivia's memories. When I can finally understand who I am.

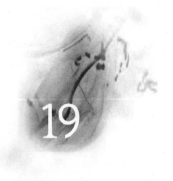

19

I wait until everyone is asleep. It doesn't take long. I don't take any pills, so the pain in my nose is enough to keep me awake.

Before I use the memory disk, I stand next to Peter's bed. He's sleeping fitfully, his fingers twitching every now and then. He makes a small noise, half of a word—he must be dreaming. It doesn't seem like a good dream, but I don't wake him from it. I stare at him in case this is the last time I ever see him. I wish my vision weren't so blurry. I touch his hair with my finger. But then my fingers are on his neck. His skin is hot from sleep, and I feel the slow and steady beat of his heart under my fingertips. He stirs, and I take my hand away, half-hoping he wakes. He doesn't, even when I kiss his temple.

I leave the KFC behind on silent feet, then step into a tiny drugstore. All of the pain medication has been stripped from the shelves by now, but I find a bottle of nasal spray. I squirt it up both nostrils until fire crackles through my sinuses and actually brings me to one knee. But it breaks up the blockage in my nose until I can breathe. I spit the stuff that comes out into a paper towel and don't look at it. Then I slam a Diet Coke for the caffeine. In the very back of the store I find a rack of cheap clothing; I take a black winter hat and the last remaining hooded sweatshirt.

I sit down in the drugstore, behind a rack full of postcards showing various shots of New York. WISH YOU WERE HERE! one says, showing the skyline on a pleasant summer day, the sun glowing between the buildings. JUSTICE FOR ALL says another, showing the Statue of Liberty. I wish that were true.

I pull the disk out of my pouch and rub my thumb over it. It's small and black and hard, and feels heavier than it looks. *What are you waiting for?* I ask myself. But I know why I'm waiting. I have no idea what this thing will do to me. I have no idea if I'll be able to handle what it shows me.

But like so many other times in my life, I don't really have a choice.

I close my eyes, reach through my hair, and stick the disk onto the base of my skull.

I feel velvety heat, and then a cool liquid sensation spreads

173

throughout my brain. I settle back against the wall. And then I learn the truth.

I don't spend too long living inside Olivia's memories. Just enough for me to understand.

Once upon a time, things were very different in True Earth. The Ruling Five could more accurately be called the Ruling Four, because the director reigned supreme. The five of them had rescued the world from the ashes of a nuclear war, but trouble was brewing once again. Olivia was discovering that humanity lived in cycles, and we were steadily marching toward a second apocalypse. For the last century, the director had been concerned with destroying external threats, rather than fixing the rising problems of True Earth itself.

Discovering my world and True Earth are one and the same was a happy accident. Three years ago from my current point in time, Olivia traveled through the Black to what she thought was another world, a world she'd been keeping close tabs on for a long while. It was going to be the next world True Earth conquered, unless she could stop them. Olivia had been fighting back against True Earth's savagery in secret for years, not daring to fight the director head-on. Olivia knew she would lose and be killed in a permanent way.

Years before, she had arrived to take Noble away, to prepare him for the invasion. At that time she had no idea about the connection between the worlds. She showed Noble the eyeless, the tool True Earth would use to conquer, and asked if he would like to rebel. He said yes.

But on this visit three years ago, as the time for the invasion grew near, she discovered something new. Olivia found the Originals living as teenagers in a small suburb of Cleveland. They were just students, with backpacks, and normal lives, and parents, and after-school activities, and friends. I see images of them throughout their day-to-day lives as Olivia studied them from afar. Olivia was witnessing herself as she was a thousand years ago. It was then she realized that True Earth was planning to invade its own past.

Had Olivia and True Earth never interfered, her own past would have played out just the way she remembered it. The teens would have carried on with their lives, not knowing that ten years later the world would be mostly destroyed by nuclear war, and civilization would break down across the globe. Only China maintained some form of government as clouds of radiation spread throughout the planet. And that only lasted for about a year. Olivia knew all this because she'd lived it.

As survivors, the group of friends traveled to China, where Olivia had family high up in what remained of the government. The years passed, and eventually they, like most of the survivors, began to suffer from the radiation that was present across much of the planet. They underwent treatment. They aged. The government broke down, and soon there was just a barren wasteland with small pockets of survivors.

But science continued. In the ruins of Beijing, a community of 567 people discovered a way to clean the air. They discovered the key to aging. Survivors didn't just heal, they grew younger. By now the Originals were leaders in the small community, and they brought this technology across the globe over the following decades.

And they began to control it.

When Olivia returned to True Earth, she decided to take action before it was too late. She didn't want to see the director destroy everything all over again, after humanity had worked so hard to survive over so many eons. She didn't want the past to repeat itself. And she was sick of standing by while True Earth destroyed any realm it considered a threat to their twisted idea of perfection.

And now she knew she could fix it.

In her effort to make True Earth what it was supposed to be, what it *had* been in the first few hundred years of its existence, Olivia decided to wipe the identities of the director and her friends as teens, including herself, and give them over to the creators with fabricated memories of a past that never happened. These new identities were based on things they'd experienced, but altered in a way to fit with our new reality.

In the future, I am not just the director, but Peter is the

Original Peter. Noah is the Original Noah. Olive is the Original Olivia. Rhys is the Original Rhys. Noah and Olive and Rhys are dead right now, but Olivia has their identities stored, ready to bring them back at the right time.

The creators had already been here for decades, thinking they were preparing for just another invasion—even they were ignorant about the truth of our world. They were just following orders, like East said. By the time Olivia first discovered our worlds were linked, the creators had lived out entire lives here, growing into the adults I would later meet.

Three years ago Olivia took us away from our lives, from our parents and friends. Before Olivia, I went to school with the Alpha team. We did normal things. We went to Friday night football games. But all of that was replaced with memories of lessons in combat and warfare, missions and exercises.

Only the last three years of Alpha team is real. We were never raised as children to be weapons. We were just children. But to Olivia, it made more sense to take us away from our original lives and to prepare us for the coming nuclear war instead. The survivors would need us to lead one day, after all.

Olivia went back to True Earth to see if the changes she made transferred into True Earth, and they had. By making the director someone she could control, her team had truly become the Ruling Five, more tightly bound than they had been in centuries. True Earth was a slightly more prosperous place, and the threat of war did not loom quite as large.

Now, when nuclear war eventually did arrive in my time, our team would be ready to take control of a broken earth. We wouldn't have to wait for the technology or the skills that would come later, like we did the first time. We wouldn't have to struggle on our way to China, avoiding roving packs of gangs intent on killing/raping/stealing everything in their path. We could take control earlier, in a more efficient way. With our organization and power, we could create the best world possible, one completely free of war and famine and rape and murder. One free of hatred and racism. We could create the truest world of all.

But then the future changed again. Because of me.

Olivia couldn't tell the others what she was doing. How could she? She was tampering with their lives, and with the future of everyone on the planet. So True Earth still invaded our world with the eyeless, and Olivia could only do her best to help me stop them, to keep things on the right track. Letting the eyeless complete their mission would've ensured there wasn't going to be any kind of future at all.

But when I defeated the eyeless, I changed the future anyway. The world was more unified afterward, and nuclear war never came to pass. The external threat of the eyeless woke everyone up and made them realize they couldn't afford to fight with one another. But no good thing lasts forever.

The result? As of right now, True Earth is a half-held-together mess of countries. The lack of a nuclear war kept us down the same path we're on right now, continuing the slow decay of our environment and culture and the depletion of almost every natural resource. The sky is black most of the time, the air unsafe to breathe. All because the Originals never took over following a nuclear war, as they were meant to. The "reset" of our world never happened, and the population continued to grow. After I destroyed the eyeless, the Originals returned to True Earth to find it was not as they had left it.

Olivia, obviously, knew why. She was finally forced to share her secret with the Originals, and the plan to invade New York began. The others haven't quite forgiven her for her deception, but after a thousand years of companionship, they weren't able to just kill her, either.

But now the director is willing to risk re-creating the effects of nuclear war in order to get back the world that they knew before, the one they worked so hard to construct. Releasing the Black will do exactly that.

Perhaps the most important thing Olivia's disk shows me is that the director doesn't want to stop us; she wants to help me and my team take control, to live the lives we're supposed to live, to eventually become the Ruling Five ourselves and create the brightest future of all.

The reality of what's ahead for me and my teammates

settles around my neck like a lead chain. But I refuse to let it weigh me down. Because it also shows me something.

There is a future, and it is anything but certain. It is changing all the time.

Olivia leaves me a final memory, one that is more the understanding of an idea than anything else.

The director doesn't know every move before I make it, because I do have free will. Things are playing out in a way they never have before.

And that means I still have a choice.

I don't know what side Olivia is on. Maybe part of her doesn't want to meddle with our world any more than she already has. Maybe she wants to let events happen as they will.

But I know part of her is still loyal to the Ruling Five and to achieving her perfect world. Because the last thing I learn is that she gave me these memories with the director's consent, as the first step to me and my team becoming who we are meant to become.

And the device feeding memories into my brain right now doubles as a homing beacon, which was activated as soon as I used it.

True Earth knows we're here. And they're coming to make sure we do our job.

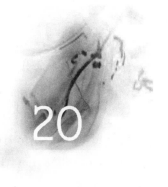

20

I come out of my trance and I'm on my feet, pain temporarily forgotten. I step out of the store and scream as loud as I can—*"Incomiüüünnnggg!"*

The warning carries through the sleeping station, and other voices repeat the words, and soon there are soldiers everywhere. I peel the stamp off the back of my head and try to crush it under my foot, but it's too strong, so I kick it underneath a vending machine.

I want to stay and fight, but we can't be taken alive. Who knows what they can do to make us follow their little plan— they may not kill us, but there are worse things than death. If abandoning these people right now means we can save more in the end, perhaps *billions* more, we have to do it.

I don't know why Olivia gave me the heads-up. Maybe she feels bad. Maybe she knows she made a mess she no longer knows how to fix.

I hobble as fast as I can back to Peter. Noble and Sophia are already there, troubled sleep all over their faces. Seeing them safe loosens the wire around my lungs just a little. I stare at Peter, trying to imagine the life he left behind. And the life I left behind. The lives that were stolen from us. I wonder what our families were like, and what they thought when we were taken away by Olivia and given to the creators.

We were friends before we were taken, when the most dangerous thing we had to worry about was school. If only there were some way to get back there. But would I give up the life I know now, would I *willingly* wipe my identity again?

Peter is staring at me funny, probably because I'm staring at him funny. "Are you okay?"

"Fine. Yes. Sorry. I'm together."

"Safe house," Noble says.

"What?" I say.

"We're going to the secondary safe house on Twenty-third Street, across from the Flatiron. The one overlooking Madison Square Park."

"Fine, let's go."

"We're just going to leave these people to fight alone?" Sophia says.

Peter shakes his head, climbing off his gurney. "Once True Earth discovers we're not here, they won't care about these people. Our being here is putting them in danger."

Sophia can't really argue with that, so we head for the exit. I'm not sure what Peter said is true, though—what's to keep them from slaughtering out of spite?

As we walk, Noble says, "We can't go in a group. Miranda, you go ahead, keep your hood up, and pretend like you're just trying to stay out of trouble. I know that's a stretch for you."

"Got it," I reply. Surprisingly, Peter nods instead of objects. I tug my hood tighter around my face, then walk in a different direction.

The guards on the escalator have left for the other side of the station. Bursts of gunfire and shouted orders come from that direction. I climb the dead escalator as fast as I can, pain flaring through all my injured parts. I'm exhausted by the time I get to the top and find my way blocked by dozens of cars piled on top of one another. The soldiers must have stacked them to create a makeshift barricade.

But one car window is open. I half crouch, look through it, and see a path through another window. The cars are arranged in such a way as to provide a path you can crawl through. A clever way to bottleneck any assault by the enemy.

I shimmy through the first window of a small red sedan. Then it's up through the window of a black SUV. It's difficult work, especially since I'm working one-handed, and I groan every time my body hits a part of a car. It's so cold I think about giving up and turning back. I can't feel my nose at all, and the swollen side of my face begins to sting.

I make it through the tangle of cars and onto the empty street. More vehicles are strewn about, some smashed together, all of them abandoned. The sky overhead is black and starless. The city still has power, but most of the lights are off, as if darkness can keep the people inside safe. The silence is crushing.

I only have ten blocks to walk, but in my current state I'm worried about getting jumped by anyone who wants my stuff, not that I really have stuff. I almost go back a second time, even slowing my pace for a moment (which is already super slow), but then I press on. After a block I find a shortcut through an alley. It's dark, as alleys usually are. I slip through a broken chain-link fence and stand in the middle of the lane, my breath coming out in huge, dim clouds. There is so little light, I can't see my fingers at arm's length.

I hear a soft footstep behind me, the crunch of a foot on snow. I whirl, and something thumps me in the hip hard enough to send me spinning to the ground, jarring every bone in my body. I don't stand up right away—the pain is too much. I grit my teeth, then push myself to my knees.

From the darkness in front of me a shadow steps forward.

184

The director is clad in her golden armor, with a thick fur coat that goes to her knees. She wears a crimson scarf wrapped delicately around her neck and a smile on her lips.

"Hello, Miranda," she says.

Well, shit.

"I wouldn't," she says softly when I try to stand up. In her right hand is a sword. She presses the point against my neck, keeping me pinned to the freezing ground.

"You wouldn't? Then we truly aren't the same person," I say.

"You viewed the memories Olivia gave you, correct?"

I nod, not taking my eyes off her.

"Then you see now how vital you and your friends are. You will need to bring this world under control, or all will truly be lost. There is really no choice."

I'm getting a little tired of hearing that. I do have a choice.

"You know we care about your future," the director continues. "Nuclear war will take this world, whether it's five years from now or twenty. Even if we weren't here now, your civilization would still end. So why does it matter *when* it happens?"

"Funny, you didn't care about our world before Olivia told you the truth, before your time got screwed up. You were ready to wipe us off the map, as you've done to so many worlds before."

She can't really defend that, and she doesn't try; she just

looks away briefly, then says, "Things change. Now we're here to make it right." She removes the tip of her sword from my neck.

Slowly, I stand up, making sure I won't suddenly fall.

The director puts her hand on my shoulder. "And you know I'm right," she says again. "Because you see the world you live in now. War, famine, corruption. Genocide. Murder and rape." The director leans in, putting her lips right against my ear, and she whispers, "What are you trying to save?"

I honestly don't know.

"I know what the future looks like. I lived it. It is more terrifying and brutal than anything we could put you through now. Why wouldn't you want to prevent that?"

I would. I would want to prevent it.

But I'd have to do it without sacrificing innocent lives.

"You know your world is toxic, and what that toxicity will lead to, in time," the director says. "Do the right thing, Miranda."

Right or wrong, I know which side I have to stand on.

And she seems to see my decision as I make it. Her eyes narrow, and I don't even have time to fight back. She cuffs me on the side of the head so hard that I'm unconscious before I hit the ground.

I wake up in the alley, seconds or minutes later, I can't really say. I'm on my back, shivering in the snow. Every few seconds, pain radiates from my right eye, branching out to the back of my skull. I groan and try to roll onto my side, but everything hurts.

The director crouches next to me, staring down into my face. Her fingers touch my cheek, gently.

"I don't expect you to accept everything right away," she says. "Or to know what's best for this world. Rest now," she continues. "Your journey is just beginning."

"Wait..." I almost ask about Peter and the others, if they've been captured too, but I don't want to give anything away. The director just stares down at me, with an expression somewhere between hope and disappointment, until the pain is too much and the blackness returns.

I wake up again warm and dry, in bed. All of my aches and pains are gone. Peter, Noble, and Sophia are in the room with me. It looks like a studio apartment. Peter is sitting next to me. Noble is standing at a table that holds a coffeepot and a pitcher of orange juice. Sophia is sitting in a chair by herself with her knees hugged to her chest.

The whole room is lit by candles and a few emergency glow stick things scattered on the floor. I'm wearing the same ragged suit of red armor.

Peter grabs my hand, squeezes it, and blinks away a few tears. "You're okay. You've been out for four days, but you're all right."

I want to cry too, but I can't feel anything besides numb. "What happened?"

Noble pours coffee into a mug. He sets the pot down a little too hard. "Four days ago we were overwhelmed. You were gone. The soldiers at Penn Station were captured or killed, and the people were sent back onto the streets. Twelve hours ago a team of Roses put us in this room with you. Four hours ago the lights went out and we were given these candles. You've been in a coma. We were told your brain was bleeding, but one of their doctors fixed it."

I take the information as it's given and don't feel a thing. I simply can't. We met some soldiers and now they're dead. Whatever resistance was forming is dead.

"Why would they put us all together? Alone?"

Noble sits beside my bed and rests his hand on my forearm. His face is heavy with grief, and I doubt he's slept much in those four days, but I still see his old warmth behind his eyes. "Because we are no longer a threat to these people. Congratulations, we lost. All you have to do is take a look outside to see that."

"They told us everything," Sophia says. "About who you

and Peter really are. Noble thinks they wanted us to know how *necessary* it is to go along with their plan."

Peter and I share a look. What can we say?

He winds his fingers through mine, and I focus on that. *Feel something.* I should feel relief we're all together, but there is something crucial missing. Hope. It's like we're all just waiting to die.

Still, I focus on the feel of his palm on the back of my hand, warm and dry and a little rough. We're still alive, and together. Things can always get worse, even if it doesn't feel that way.

"You have to stop scaring me," Peter whispers in my ear. I just look at him. There's no witty retort this time.

Something feels off about the way Peter's holding my hand. Then I remember my injury. I gently pull my hand free and hold it up in front of me. I have a new scar in my palm that twists up through to the tip of my little finger. It looks like it's been healed for a few weeks, but I can tell that at one point it was burst completely open. I just keep staring at it, unable to bend my little finger all the way. The healing process was clearly sped along somehow, like the time Dr. Delaney fixed my broken nose (which also seems to be fixed for the second time).

No one says anything. Peter just takes my hand again and holds it against the bed.

"They turn on the TV every now and then," Peter says.

"They show us the news. But the last time was almost, what, six hours ago?"

Noble sips his coffee and shrugs. "Thereabouts."

"Six hours." Peter nods, like he's glad he was able to confirm something. As if it's a small victory. *Hey, we figured out how much time has passed, maybe we can figure a way out of here.*

"And we're still alive because the director needs Peter and me," I say. "Because she needs us to put the future back on track."

"She doesn't *need* anyone," Noble spits, but then his harsh look softens. "So she is you in the future. That means nothing. She could get any one of her clones to rebuild this world. She could do it herself if she wanted to. But the Originals are intent on making things a certain way. You're still alive—*we're* still alive because she thinks she can convince you to do what she wants."

Sophia lifts her head suddenly. "If you're her, then we should kill you," she says plainly.

I look at her, and she looks right back at me. I shrug. She's right.

"Jesus!" Peter stands up. "Nobody is killing anyone. If you did, you'd have to kill me too. Don't you see? Miranda still has a choice. If this is a new time line, then Miranda can do whatever she wants. The director is holding the entire world hostage, but Miranda has a *choice*. We all do."

"It's true," I say. "Nothing is predetermined."

"All I know is Rhys is dead," Sophia says. "And he died to save her."

Peter shakes his head. "But is he really? It sounds like all our identities are stored somewhere. Even Noah's, and especially Olive's."

"Yes, Peter, he is dead," Sophia says sharply. "I saw him die, if you've forgotten."

"Let's remember we are almost certainly being watched," Noble says.

"We led them right to East," Sophia says quietly.

Noble rubs his forehead. "That's enough, please."

I stare into Peter's eyes, which appear black in the yellowish candlelight, and want to fall right into them. They're still warm. Somehow I know they'll always be warm when they look at me. "East told me"—my mouth tastes and feels like it's full of cotton balls—"that if we didn't get him out, everything was lost."

"Like I said, take a look outside," Noble says.

I slide out of bed, my healed skin feeling tight in places, but good overall.

Sophia starts talking again, but I ignore her. I leave the apartment, following glow sticks up a series of steps. Peter follows at a distance behind me. I climb a few flights of stairs, relishing the feeling in my stiff muscles, a good kind of pain.

At the top of the stairs the door to the roof is broken. I step out and walk to the edge, the air even colder than it was before. The building is located on the east side of Central Park, overlooking the Verge and the wide swath of crushed and burned trees around it.

Peter comes up beside me, and together we just stare at the Verge. There is no longer a laser coming out of the top. Instead there's a thick beam of Black, firing straight up into the sky and spreading out in all directions. It makes no sound; there is no sound anywhere. It's too late. True Earth got the Key, and they've used it on our world to recreate the effects of a nuclear war. We got up here just in time to watch the end.

As more Black spills into the sky and spreads like an upside-down puddle, lights still glowing in the city flicker and die. Whole buildings lose power, one after another, until there is no light to see by. I can't even see Peter, but I reach for him in the dark and press my lips to his.

"We can still keep fighting," he says, but I'm not interested in hearing words anymore. "Fighting in a different way. Maybe bringing order to the world right now is the best thing we can do."

I don't know what to say to that, so I say nothing.

Sophia and Noble join us after a while, and then together we go back to the room.

Where Olivia is waiting for us.

21

Olivia sits casually in a chair next to the desk, her legs crossed.

"Tell us what's happening out there," Noble says, both of his hands in fists. "Tell us something."

Olivia licks her lips. She looks . . . *ashamed*. And she should be. This mess is her fault. It was her desire to meddle, not the director's. If only she had let events play out like they were supposed to. No matter how horrific they might've been, they would've been *natural*.

"Tell us!" Noble says.

"The director used the Key to cripple your world. No one is capable of fighting back now." *East—what did she do to him?*

"What does that mean?" Peter says.

"She used the Key to manipulate the Black, harnessing the energy to burn out every electronic device across the globe. Your world is dark now, like it was in the days after the war. It's morning outside, but the sun is hidden behind the Black. And will be for as long as it's here."

Another ten seconds go by where no one says anything. I try to imagine what it's like out there, and I can't. Seven billion people in a world of darkness. Pitch-black. Like being trapped in a nightmare.

"Why?" Noble says.

"Because now no one can fight back. It's over."

"This is it," I say. "This is how she'll rebuild. Billions will die, and those who survive will be part of the world moving forward."

This is when I'm supposed to take control of the entire world, along with my team. We're back in the Dark Ages. Only we have the power now.

"What about the rest of my team? Noah, Rhys...you."

Olivia stands up. "They will be here in a few days. They may not... *I* may not remember things you all remember. Some of their memories could not be saved, but they will more or less be your teammates. We will ... *You* will all be together again."

Noble gasps, and Sophia claps a hand over her mouth. I know they're thinking of Rhys. We lost him so recently, and the thought of him returning before we've even had time to grieve is incomprehensible. Would it just be normal, like he took a quick vacation?

I flex my left hand, rubbing my thumb over the new scar. "Why did you come here, Olivia?"

"To summon you. The director plans to have you speak directly to the world before the day is over. You're to meet her outside."

Oh, no big deal, she just wants me to speak directly to the world.

"What about the rest of us?" Sophia says.

"You will remain here." I think she wants to say more, but all she ends up saying is, "I'm sorry."

Olivia opens the door and leaves, but not before opening the fingers of her left hand and dropping something on the floor.

It's a crumpled ball of paper. I make it there before anyone else and raise my hand for silence. I unfold the ball and hold it flat against my palm. It reads,

They are listening. Meet me downstairs.

And then, below that,

There is hope.

The warmth flooding through my limbs must be exactly that—hope. I pass the note around, holding a finger to my lips. Maybe Olivia is having a change of heart. Or maybe it's just another ruse. I don't think I'll ever be able to fully trust her again.

Peter takes the finger away so he can kiss me.

Noble just nods. I leave them all behind.

I find Olivia in the shadow of a stairwell. We're in an apartment building with fancy, super expensive-looking décor. Roses are everywhere, carrying sticks that glow as bright as torches. Shadows play off the walls, highlighted by green and gold light. The Roses are all moving with purpose, some carrying supply boxes, a few carrying weapons. Clearly this was a backup base separate from the Verge, but now they're leaving; I can't tell if that's good or bad.

No one looks at me twice, but I know I can't just walk out of here. The director isn't that stupid.

"What's going on?" I whisper to Olivia.

"We're leaving. The invasion force is scaling down to an occupation force." She stops when two Roses look in our direction briefly, then pretend they didn't see us once they recognize her. I guess lurking in the stairwell isn't exactly inconspicuous.

"Why are you telling me this?" I can't keep the edge out of my voice.

"A group of soldiers is being held in the camp in Central

Park. They're currently freezing to death, along with many others, but if someone were to free them..."

"Why would I believe anything you say?"

She steps closer, in my face now. "In exactly one hour, go three blocks south and two blocks east, then enter the restaurant with the broken window. I'll be there." She squeezes my arm once, then slips in with the moving Roses, instantly becoming just another Olivia, albeit one wearing golden armor.

I don't know what game she's playing. All I know is I'm supposed to meet the director right now, and I don't want to disappoint her.

22

I find the director outside, facing away from the building, arms folded across the small of her back. The sky is alive with Axes, the light from their engines standing out against the darkness. The windows in every building are dark; I see only one distant fire burning orange with people-shapes moving around it. The dim form of the Verge is visible in the distance, its metallic surface reflecting what light there is, but the ruins of the Time Warner Center are hidden in gloom. The snow is coming down again, thick and fast.

The only reason I can see the director is that she has five Roses around her holding electric torches. It makes them all glow a ghastly greenish-gold, highlighting the blowing snow like sparks.

I stop a few feet away, and she turns around, giving me a big, creepy smile I would never make on purpose. "You look healthier."

"Thanks."

"I assume you're here because you're ready to begin?"

"You haven't left me much choice."

"Actually I've left you one."

The wind howls, kicking snow up between us. It swirls sideways, stinging my face. I'd like to be anywhere else in the world right now. The bastards couldn't have waited until summer to invade?

"Okay . . ." I say.

"You can either do what you're supposed to and unite with your team. Or you can continue to fight me, your very self, and I will alter history further by replacing you with another Miranda clone who will get the job done. You will die again, and when you come back, you will be different . . . but the result will be the same. We are prepared to pull the strings from a distance if it means securing the future of this planet. So you can either do your part to recover from *this*"—she points to the sky—"or you let us experiment with other versions of you. Either way, this won't end. People will die."

I stare at her in silence.

"Do you really want to stand by and do nothing? I wouldn't, so I assume you wouldn't, either."

She's right; I don't want to.

"What would I have to do?"

She nods. "For now, all you have to do is wait. While the animals eat one another."

I shiver, thinking about what that looks like around the world right now. Humanity is gripped in more terror than anything an army of Roses could have caused. Everything is just . . . gone. We've failed. No matter what comes next, we've failed. The best we can hope for is to turn out like Commander Gane's world.

"Your team will spend the next year in the Verge, or anywhere else in the city you prefer. Consider yourself free. Soon the Black will be sealed. Within weeks, the darkness will be lifted and you will see the sun again, but there will be no power, no running water, for a very long time. Use the next year to bring this city under your control. Establish order, and I know you will be ready to lead. I will return after that year and give you the gift of immortality. Then your team will truly be on the path to taming the world."

"Why do you trust me?" I say.

She sighs through her nose. "Because I *am* you. And I know you want to do what's right."

She takes a moment, peering into the darkness around us. "I will be glad to go home, to see what changes have occurred after all this, if any." She settles her gaze on me again. "I can see in your eyes that you're only now beginning to understand what you must do. And accept."

It's true. If we don't do what they order, they'll just try to figure something else out. Maybe going as far as giving us the tattoos they used to control Beta team. We will simultaneously be ourselves and not ourselves. So what am I supposed to do?

"Your team will join you in the Verge," the director says softly. "Your *whole* team."

I can't deny that seeing my friends again makes me tremble in a way that's not so terrible. I miss them so much. I miss being a family. I miss feeling like we're doing something good, and right.

"Good-bye for now," she says. "Be in the Verge by noon. That's four hours from now. From there you will address the world."

The director starts to leave, heading toward the Verge with her crew.

"What am I supposed to say?" I call after her.

She considers this, then shrugs. "Whatever you think they need to hear. This is your show now, Miranda. The world is counting on you." She turns away.

I stand in the ice and cold for a few more minutes, feeling the darkness and the silence around me. Someone screams somewhere very far away, or maybe it's just the wind.

I want to cry for the people dying right now. For the people who will die in five minutes, five hours. For those who will make it five days in this dark new world.

I want to cry for them, but there is work to do.

I go back into the building and find my team in the apartment. They all turn to look when the door opens. I stare back at them, not knowing where to begin.

"Here's what happens next," I say, and then I tell them what we're supposed to do.

"But we're not going to do that," Sophia says.

"If we don't, it's over," Peter says. "Did you miss that part? We had our chance. Now it's time to think about what we can do to save the most lives."

"Have we had our chance, though?" I ask. "It sounds like we have one more."

Noble's eyes are a little clearer. He's holding something small and black in his hand. "I found the bug, but there may be more. Shall we ... ?" He gestures to the hall.

We leave the room, go up two flights of stairs, and kick in one of the apartment doors. It's a posh space with antique furniture everywhere and no occupants. The Roses must've cleared the whole building out when they took it over.

I tell them what Olivia said about meeting with us.

"She's up to something," Noble said. "We can't trust her. It could be a trap."

"Clearly," Sophia says.

"Listen," I say. "If we fight back, we need to hit hard."

"A surgical strike, yes," Noble says. "But we don't even know where East is being held. He's the Key, so without him, we can't change a thing. And even if we do find him, there's no guarantee we can change anything at all! The Key could be destroyed, or rendered inert by using it—East might even be dead. So do we trust Olivia, or go off on our own?"

"I think we might have to trust her," I say. "Carefully."

"What is the point of fighting?" Peter says. "The damage is done. We can do more good here, if we try. I don't know if we have the right to gamble with so many lives. Maybe surrendering is the right path." I never thought I'd hear him say that. Could he be right?

"No, it's not. We can keep them from doing this to the next world," Sophia says, brow furrowed. "Let's not forget where I came from. They aren't going to suddenly stop traveling through the Black, wiping out other universes. *Other* lives will be affected by our inaction, not just the ones here."

"Let's see what Olivia is up to," I say, wandering into the kitchen. "If it's a trap, it's a trap. We can't be much worse off than we are already. If it's not a trap, we need her help." I drink two glasses of rusty-tasting water. The fridge has leftovers, some ham in a plastic container and what smells like gouda mashed potatoes. I stare at them, thinking, *Rhys would be all over those right now.* So would Noah.

That's when I know this isn't a question of fighting back. *Of course* we fight back. Rhys and Noah wouldn't roll over and take the director's orders if they were alive and we weren't.

Peter comes in and eats a piece of ham. A few minutes pass as we just eat and look at the floor, but then I'm looking at him, because he's easy to look at, and because I know he could be taken away from me again at any time.

As if he can hear what I'm thinking, he puts his hand on my shoulder. Then he pulls me to his chest.

"I'm really looking forward to spending some normal time together," he says.

"God, me too."

"I missed you so much," he says. "You don't even know."

"Not as much as I missed you."

"When it's over, if we're alive, we're going to go on vacation."

"Oh, tell me more," I whisper against his neck.

"We're going to go to a beach, and we'll swim with dolphins and collect seashells. Actually I don't care about collecting seashells, but I definitely want to swim with dolphins. And then we'll go into the mountains and get a cabin and hunt mountain lions."

"I like mountain lions."

"I know, me too. We'll hunt them to capture them and make them our pets."

I smile, and the smile turns into a laugh. But soon the moment is gone. He kisses me once on the forehead and whispers in my ear, "I love you. No matter what happens next."

I carry that with me as we wait out the hour. We even curl up on the couch and catch a quick nap. It's nice. And normal.

But then Noble is gently shaking us awake. "It's time," he says. He opens his jacket and yanks out a panel hidden in the fake fur. Inside are capped syringes filled with the familiar yellow liquid. "Better safe than sorry," Noble says. "With so much going on, we can't forget about the small stuff."

"Thanks for taking care of us," I say to him. "You're a genius."

He shrugs, smiling. "What can I say?"

Peter goes to the bathroom, and Noble removes one more syringe from his jacket. This one is filled with a deeper yellow fluid, closer to honey. "Keep this on you, Miranda. If you come across a group of Roses, I want you to try using your power. You won't send them running, but you may . . . disorient them. Startle, at the very least."

"How is that possible? Roses are immune to fear waves."

He looks away. "I was able to modify you slightly while you were in your tank, which will let you tolerate a shot this strong and may allow your power to work on other Roses. I'm sorry for tampering—I hope you're not upset—but if we were going to bring you back, I wanted to give you an edge." His eyes fall to the new syringe. "Your power should work, at least a little. But you must take this shot soon after. It's very important. Wait too long and you could burn out. You could literally forget everything on the spot. And possibly go into a coma. Or worse."

"Well at least you're not scaring me." The syringe has a metal strip, so I touch it to the small of my back and it sticks to the magnetic scales.

"I'm sorry, I—" Noble begins.

I stand and squeeze his wrist. "Thank you."

He nods. "Use your judgment. You always have." I can tell he wants to say more.

"I miss him too."

Noble stares at my hand on his wrist, and his eyes shimmer all at once. "He loved you, you know. Like a sister. He would check on you when you were in the tank. *I'm going to visit Miranda,* he would say."

All I can do is nod.

Soon we're back in the cold, which scours the remaining sleep from our bones. To the south, a building is on fire, offering just enough reddish light to see by. I see a few people walking down the street with oil-burning lanterns they must've stolen from some outdoor supply store.

"Let's move," Noble says.

We do, jogging the five blocks to the restaurant slowly, eyes peeled for danger. We pass a few people on the street who huddle in doorways or shattered storefronts. The jog has almost warmed me up by the time we reach the final intersection. The sushi restaurant across the street has a big hole right in the front window, like someone tossed a brick clean through.

Then I feel a rumble through the soles of my feet. "Cover!" Noble whispers, and we all dive behind a parked SUV. A Thorn rips down the street, kicking up a rooster tail of snow. It's there and gone. We wait a few more seconds, listening hard, then sneak up to the side of the sushi restaurant.

We push through the front door. It's not any warmer inside, but the air is still. Olivia is sitting at a table near the bar in the back. We walk over and sit down like we're having dinner together. It's eerily quiet.

"Is there any food left?" Sophia says as a hello.

Olivia folds her hands on the table. "It's all gone. Just one bottle of sake that had rolled under a cupboard."

"Let's get down to business," Noble says. "Why did you call us here?"

"And why should we trust you?" I add. Looking at her,

I still can't believe she's the girl I fought side by side with in the forest after Tycast died and the Beta team came after us. I watched her die at the top of Key Tower, and yet here she is, a thousand years older, not the person I knew at all.

"Because I've had a change of heart," she says. "Perhaps I don't want to tinker with fate any longer. We've made a mess, and I thought this was the right way to fix it, but it's possible I've lost perspective. Since I no longer know what the right thing to do is, I've decided that maybe this is..."

"Wrong," Sophia finishes for her.

It sounds too good to be true. "How can you help us?" I say.

She allows a small smile, one I remember so well. "Our forces decrease by the second. We're returning home, for now. But you have survivors in this city who are prepared to fight. Not long ago, a group of prisoners were brought into the park. Men dressed as soldiers—"

"Kellogg and his men," Peter says. "Of course."

"And they're actually still alive?" Sophia says. Her dark eyes are narrowed.

"They are," Olivia says.

My heart begins to race. If we free those men, we'll have an assault force—a small one, but a group of trained soldiers none-theless. I could show up to address the world with an army.

"What would we do with them?" Noble says. "We need

the Key, which is probably in a different universe. That means finding East. Do you know if he's still alive?"

Olivia nods. "East has wired the Key to his central nervous system, quite ingeniously, I might add. It means that for the Key to be used, East has to remain alive."

"But where is he?" Noble says. "True Earth?"

"No. In order for the Key to work, it must remain in the universe it is affecting."

Which means...

Olivia smiles again, bigger this time. "East is still here."

23

Coming up with a plan to free the prisoners doesn't take too long after that. Everyone has a job. Mine is transportation. With the failure of all things electrical, we have to get a little creative. Peter thinks we might be able to get a diesel engine to work, but Noble shuts that down quickly, claiming it'd be too loud and too slow to be effective against any Thorns/Axes in the area.

Sophia brings up a great point. "Say we do get the Key. Somehow. What then? The Black has already been released."

"Once you have the Key," Olivia says, "you just have to travel through the Black and you'll end up in a special room. From there, you can begin the process of removing the Black. Power restoration will follow shortly thereafter. Right now, electrical fields are suppressed. Our vehicles are shielded from the effects. Forget radio transmission too."

"Maybe we can spend a few years reverse-engineering their tech, if all else fails," Peter says dryly.

No one laughs, but I don't think he expected anyone to.

We rise together, and Noble reaches across the table to shake Olivia's hand. "Thank you. We needed this."

"I hope it's not too late," she says. "I still don't know what's right, but I think I've broken things enough by trying to fix them."

Outside there are no Roses in sight, since their purpose here has been fulfilled, but that doesn't mean there aren't any around . . . or that people won't recognize us as clones.

"We need to blend in," I say.

"Agreed," Peter says. "Look."

Across the street is a sporting goods store, the windows helpfully shattered already. Inside most of the clothing is gone, the hangers lying around like discarded bones. Smart people stocking up for the long winter, I guess. Or maybe they just wanted free stuff. We find enough clothing for all of us, though. Sophia takes a big silver puffy jacket, and I find several long-sleeve T-shirts I can layer, a thick black scarf, and a pair of waterproof overalls that somehow fit perfectly. I look like I'm ready to go inner-tubing rather than fight a war. Noble already looks the part, so he just grabs a big flannel hat with ear flaps.

Peter puts on a pink hat with little eyeholes, clearly meant for a kid. "How do I look?"

I laugh, and immediately feel bad. It doesn't seem right. I should be somber at all times.

But Peter laughs too, and he throws the hat at me. Somehow he knew I needed that break.

"Listen!" Noble says.

Outside a bunch of people start shouting. We duck into the shadows, behind the racks, and watch a group of at least twenty men marching down the street, holding up torches. They're definitely not from True Earth. Two of them break off and stick their heads into the store. They leave a moment later when they see there isn't much left to steal.

"Animals..." Peter says.

"People," Sophia replies.

They march onward, and no Axes show up to scatter them. Olivia was right—the force is scaling down. That means this is the end, happening right now in front of us. People will soon be devouring one another in the long night.

I creep closer to the door. The gang happens upon a man on the other side of the street, and they surround him, pulling off his jacket and the layer under it. They rip a bag full of canned food out of his arms and throw it down, the cans rolling out to be picked up by fast and greedy hands. The man falls to his knees, crunching the snow.

I step out into the street. "Miranda!" Noble says harshly. I look back, but Peter only nods at me, then moves to follow.

"No. Stay here," I say. "I just want to talk to them. If we all go, it'll become a brawl."

I walk toward the gang, my blood hot. The director was right. Somebody has to maintain order, or all that will be left are corpses.

"Hey!" I say, loud enough for the crowd to hear me. I'm dressed in my new clothes and am so bundled up, they don't recognize me as a Rose. A few of the guys stop stripping the man of all his worldly possessions and stare at me. They alert the others (I catch a muttered whisper—"Hey, look at this"), and soon the group is walking toward me slowly, spreading out to box me in on both sides. It reminds me so much of the way eyeless move that the hair on the back of my neck stands up.

It's clear who the leader is; he's the one closest to me, right in the middle. His eyes rove over me like I'm merchandise.

"Give us your clothes," the leader says.

"Better yet, let's take her with us," the shorter one next to him says.

"No," the leader says. "Too many mouths to feed. Give us your clothes."

"You have ten seconds to give that man back his stuff, and then I will let you leave in peace."

The guys look at one another and laugh. When the leader

213

sees I'm not going to give up my clothes, he steps closer, chest out, trying his best to intimidate. All I see are targets.

I could use my power here. I could scare them all to death with my mind, literally. But I don't want to do that. It's not worth needing an extra memory shot sooner.

Instead I wait until the leader's close enough—then I drive a straight punch into his nose. I feel it split under my knuckles, like cracking open a nut. He falls backward without trying to catch his balance, out cold. The snow saves his skull from breaking.

"Take him and go," I say to the others.

They don't. I sigh. I look at the clothing store, where Peter stands with Noble and Sophia. They're coming toward me, but I give a quick shake of my head and they slow, not stopping completely. I may have just punched the guy, but this can still end with words. If we can't stop the Black, these people will have a hard enough time surviving without broken limbs and open wounds.

"I know this is hard," I tell the group, "but try to stay human." Good advice for anyone, even myself.

"We'll die," one says.

"Then die well." My brain is getting hotter, and I release the pressure with a tiny pulse of fear, just enough to send them on their way. They keep their wits but disperse like I told them to. Only two guys think to grab their former leader. They carry him away, disappearing into the darkness.

I gather up the cans of food and return them to the man, who has recovered one of his jackets. The shopping bag is torn and wet, but I crumple it down well enough to hold the cans.

"Where did you get these?" I ask him.

"A store down the way. It was all they had left. Please, my family..."

"Go to them. Stay off the street if you can."

He nods graciously, almost bowing, and starts down the sidewalk. My eyes follow him, spotting more pinpricks of torches in the distance. More gangs, maybe. More pirates, thieves, looters.

"Why did you help him?" Noble says when he's gone. "We shouldn't have been in the open like that."

"Why did you help me?" Sophia says to him. "When you could've kept walking." I remember the story Sophia told when we rode to the market in her world. About how Noble saved her life. What he had saved her from.

"This is only the beginning," Peter says. "That Key better be able to turn the power back on."

I don't have much to say about it. I don't know what the world will look like in the next hour, the next day, or the next week. We can only do our best.

"Let's move," I say.

It's not until we're five minutes away from the group that I realize one of them looked very, very familiar.

One of them looked like Albin.

"I think we're being watched," I say.

"Then let's get it done," Noble replies.

The darkness provides easy cover. As we move west across the island, we're plunged into a darkness so deep I can only see ten feet in front of me. Beyond that, gray outlines become black.

Soon we're in the park, and the Verge appears out of the darkness like the prow of a ship cutting through fog. Or, in this case, snow. There's some activity around it, the rumble of vehicles, and the outlines of figures moving with purpose. We give it a wide berth.

We split up near the west border of the park, at a series of huge rocks that look like mountains in the darkness. To the south I see the tall fence of the makeshift prison where Kellogg's soldiers—and many others—are being kept. Behind the fence I can just make out people huddled together in silence against the cold. A few fires are lit inside the perimeter to keep the prisoners from actually freezing to death. Olivia seems to be telling the truth—so far.

Peter, Sophia, and Noble will go that way. But my destination lies to the north. I take a winding trail up a hill, and then down it, feeling my way through the dark with my hands out. Branches snag at my hair and scrape over my clothes. The trail dumps me at a huge barn butted up against an access road. It's one of the stables they use for the horses that give carriage rides in Central Park. With no other transportation, this is our only hope for when the time comes to move fast. Luckily I have some experience with horses.

I creep toward the dark barn, listening for movement inside. It's completely silent, no soft horse sighs or snorts. I slide the door open, and someone points a shotgun at my face.

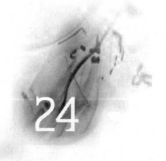

24

"What are you doing here?"

It's a woman's voice, her face hidden in the deep shadows of the barn. The shotgun is close enough for me to grab, but I don't want it to go off in the struggle.

"I need a horse," I say, figuring honesty is the best policy. "Several horses. We're mounting a counterattack."

"Who is *we*?" she says. "Get your hands up."

I get them up and slowly step back.

The woman moves with me, stepping into the soft orange light from a distant fire. She's wearing some kind of park uniform—I can't tell what color it is—and a baseball cap over light-colored hair.

"You're one of them," she says flatly.

"I am. But I'm different. Otherwise you'd be dead."

"Different how?" she asks.

"How long do you have?"

She doesn't have much time, apparently. "Get moving and I won't kill you right now. You're not taking any of my food or any of my horses."

She's about to step back inside and shut the door, I know it. And then we'll be stuck on foot.

My words come out in a tumble. "Please. Lady. I don't know a single thing for certain, except that I don't want our world to die the way it's dying right now. I need your help. Please. Help me."

What feels like a full minute passes. I exhale puffy clouds the color of chalk, and the woman does the same. The end of her shotgun barrel is dipping and swaying.

"The horses are all dead," she says. "There's just a foal I'm trying to keep alive. Along with myself."

Then she lowers the shotgun. "But I have something better." She steps back into the barn. "Come in."

I do, waiting for my eyes to adjust. Everything stays black. I hear a match strike, and then see a painful burst of yellow to the right. The woman lights a candle.

"My name is Natalie. What's yours?"

"Miranda North."

"Nice to meet you. Come with me."

I follow her past open stables, most of which are empty. Two have dead horses inside, their bodies frozen stiff on the colorless hay.

"The cold didn't kill them," Natalie says in a small, hard voice. "Their caretakers split when everything went to hell, and they had no water."

"I'm sorry." The sight turns my stomach, but a small, cynical voice inside me says at least they don't have to suffer through the coming hours/days/weeks, because they're already dead. We should all be so lucky.

"Don't be. Now they don't have to be miserable and over-worked. They've gone to the big pasture in the sky, slaves no more."

I'm already sad I have to leave Natalie behind.

We reach the end of the barn, where the foal is buried under a mound of blankets. A few candles are lit around it, carefully contained so as not to set the hay on fire.

Natalie opens the other side of the barn, revealing more dark trees and a large, dark mound. "I found it last night," she continues. "It looks abandoned, but I don't want to touch it. I'm afraid they'll come back for it."

"What is it?" My curiosity is piqued.

"Let your eyes adjust."

I step outside and the flicker from the candles fades from

my retinas. I can see an outline more clearly now against the trees. It's just a few dozen feet away. The outline is a shape I already know well.

It's one of True Earth's Axes.

"Do you know how to use it?" Natalie asks me.

"No. But I can learn pretty fast."

I walk closer to the Ax, and the details sharpen. It's covered in a light dusting of snow.

"I don't see many of them in the sky anymore," Natalie says. "Before, they were flying overhead all the time."

"That's a good thing."

"Okay, I did you a favor. And I didn't blow your head off with my shotgun. So tell me what's happening out there. I want to know what this is about."

I turn to Natalie. "Some people don't think we deserve to live. That's all there is to it, really."

"Ah. Well, screw 'em."

"You shouldn't stay here."

She shrugs. "Got nowhere else to go. My building has no water, no heat. I've seen people on every street bringing in pots of snow to melt. Thank God for the snow." I remember wishing they'd invaded during the summer, but the snow is saving lives. And I was concerned about comfort. "Maybe if you form this resistance of yours, I'll come along."

Gunfire booms in the distance, two shots, followed by a

burst of crackling automatic fire. "Guess you better get on," Natalie says. "I don't have insurance on that thing, so be careful."

She grins at me; I can just make out the glow of her smile.

I squeeze her hand. "The world is going to need people like you. Stay alive."

She hefts the shotgun. "Doing my best."

Natalie goes back into the barn and kneels next to the foal before sliding the door shut with her boot. I have a feeling I'll never see her again.

To the south, a new source of light glows bright orange. An enormous fire.

And also my cue.

I step onto the front of the Ax, between the two vertical engines. The cockpit dome beeps, and a red light passes over my face. It beeps again, and the cockpit opens, sliding backward into the vehicle. There are benefits to having a face like mine.

I sit down in the left seat, behind the controls. There is a seat next to me, and two behind. Perfect. The Ax is set up much like the Thorn, actually. I grab the two control sticks, and the dashboard lights up with a gentle hum. The dome slides back in place, cutting me off from the deathly cold air. It's so much warmer already I just want to sit here and enjoy it, but that's not happening. I take another few minutes to look over the relatively simple controls. There are no foot pedals, and the two control sticks can be pushed or pulled in any direction, including up and down.

"Please work," I say, then press the yellow button on the dash. The Ax starts up right away, all four engines spinning and glowing with soft yellow light. It lifts a foot off the ground, feeling perfectly stable. A map on the console glows a soft blue, showing all of Manhattan and most of Brooklyn. Two dots appear on the map—an Ax near Wall Street and one in Harlem.

Time to find out what the control sticks do. I pull up on them, and my stomach drops as the Ax shoots straight up, the engines rising in pitch. Suddenly I can see the fire clearly at the south end of the park next to the wreckage of the Time Warner Center.

I take a second, looking around in all directions.

The radio clicks, and a voice fills the cockpit. "State your number," an Olivia says. The Ax in Harlem lights up on the map when she talks.

"M-96," I say.

"Thank God," the other Ax transmits—a Rhys. "Someone else gets left behind." His tone is so much like my Rhys's I actually smile. It dies on my face a second later.

"Can you believe it?" the Olivia says. "This must be our punishment for something."

"Can't believe it," I say, which is actually true.

I don't say anything else, and neither do they, so I just push both sticks forward slowly, and the Ax moves toward the camp. The next second I'm there, and I have to pull back on the sticks because I've overshot the fence. The floor of the Ax is transparent from the inside, so I can see the people scatter beneath me.

Once I'm in position on the right side of the fence, I descend, careful to avoid the trees around me. I stop a few feet off the ground, then push forward slowly, bumping up against the fence. There is a slight resistance, but then it screeches and folds over like a piece of paper.

What happens next happens fast. The prisoners don't need to be told what to do. I back the Ax up, and soon the hole in the fence is filled with people. They flood through the opening, running as fast as they can. Many of them are immediately lost to darkness. My eyes skim over them, watching for a specific group. The soldiers will be together, maintaining order no matter what. I set the Ax down a safe distance away, then open the canopy. That's when I see him.

"Kellogg!" I scream.

He turns toward me, then surrounds me with his men, the same way the street gang did just a little while ago.

I hold my hands up, palms out. "It's me. It's Miranda. I opened the gate."

"I saw," he says. "What's your plan?"

"Get to safety. Form a resistance. Recover East."

"Can you be more specific?"

"Not right now. But we know East is in the Verge, and we need to get him. I was hoping you could help."

"I think we can work something out. But first we get to safety like you said. We'll take the tunnels north as far as we can to regroup."

"What about spiders?" I say. Kellogg's men are already moving out, filtering into the nearby trees. I don't know how we'll all stay together in the dark, but maybe it's better that way.

"We'll kill any we come across—there's a cache of weapons nearby that will help us do exactly that. Help me recover them."

"I'll give you a ride," I say, "but I need to find my people first."

He nods, then moves toward the passenger seat of the Ax. The fire to the south is blazing now—a distraction caused by Peter, Sophia, and Noble—but I'm not sure how many Roses are left to distract. The world is free now, free to live or die by its own strengths. We just have to make sure it lives.

We take off as people are still leaving the camp, then fly into the Upper West Side, staying as low as possible. According to the map, the other two airborne Axes are still in the same general areas as before. Seeing me head north, the Rhys says, "Ninety-six, what are you doing? Did you get that last transmission about the fire?"

"Checking on it," I say, hoping that buys me some time. I switch off the comm so they can't hear me, then set the Ax down in our meeting location next to Lincoln Center, just to the north of what used to be the Time Warner Center.

The downward thrust from my forward left engine flips over one of those tiny cars that doesn't seem like a car. "Oops."

"Teenage drivers," Kellogg says lightly. He scans the area, checking all around us for signs of movement. "We're sitting ducks here. They're going to see you aren't checking on anything."

"I'm not leaving my team. We'll just have to hope they can't leave their positions."

"You are bold as brass," he says.

"Is brass so bold?"

Kellogg sighs but says no more.

It takes ten minutes for my team to catch up. They approach with caution, using cars for cover.

"It's me!" I call out. Once they see me with Kellogg, they break from cover and jog over.

"Nice ride," Sophia says, actually smiling.

Peter grins at me too. "I call shotgun."

Noble is all business. "The camp is clear. The Roses on the

ground investigated the fire as planned, but they won't be far behind now. We need to move."

"Kellogg was telling me about a weapons cache not far from here," I say.

Kellogg nods. "That's right. Arming ourselves is priority."

"We'll need those, absolutely," Noble says, walking toward the back of the Ax. "But these will help too." He opens a panel in the back, revealing some kind of storage trunk. Inside six RAWs are neatly lined up. "As backups, these won't be coded to any specific user's armor."

I hear a familiar sound right then—an Ax approaching—so I grab the first RAW and crank the knob up to ten. Then I point it at the sky. Two seconds later, the Ax swerves around a building at the fifth story, slowing to a hover.

The Rhys's voice comes through a speaker. "Kneel and put your hands on top of—"

I fire the RAW, and the Ax explodes. One second it's all there, the next it's a giant ball of orange-black fire, sinking straight down to the street. One of the engines is still spinning, and it breaks loose, tumbling upward through somebody's window. The rest of the Ax crashes to the ground.

Everyone else takes a RAW, including Kellogg, which leaves one left in the Ax.

"I'm going to regroup with my men at the cache," Kellogg says. "After that we'll move through the subway tunnels all the way north. I know my apartment in Washington Heights has generators, and the super will play it smart with the fuel. We fall back there and come up with a solid plan."

"What about all the people we just set loose?" I say. "We can't let them just wander in the cold."

"That's exactly what everyone else is doing. Many of them will go home. Once I'm with my men, we'll corral anyone who wants to make the trip north. We'll need more men than I have if we're going to assault anything. And they'll be safer with us."

"Because the people were so safe at Penn Station," Sophia says.

Kellogg's lip twitches. "And whose fault was that? They knew where we were because of *you*."

"Don't blame all of us...." She stops herself, probably realizing I'm the only one to blame. She isn't wrong. "Didn't we just rescue you?"

"A rescue implies safety afterward," Kellogg says. "Eight-oh-four West One hundred nintieth Street. It's a hike. Be there."

In the end, Noble and Sophia go with Kellogg to assist, and I go with Peter in the Ax. It sounds like a decent plan—the Ax will certainly come in handy—but all good feelings go out the window when I turn the thing on.

The map shows twenty airborne Axes. All of them converging on our location.

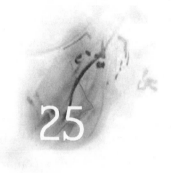

25

"Those dots are bad, right?" Peter says.

"Hold on," I say. The canopy slams shut and then we're airborne, swooping around the corner and heading north on Broadway. The other Axes are seconds away at most. They have training, I don't, and I'm supremely outnumbered, so there's really only one avenue of escape. One that might be too crazy for them to take themselves. I fly us up, rising to the tenth or eleventh floor of the buildings on either side.

"Miranda, I don't think— Look!"

Two Axes have rounded the corner of the block at the far end. They're coming straight at us.

"Turn around!" Peter says, but there's no time. They'll chase us and shoot us down. I rotate the Ax ninety degrees until I'm facing the window of an office building. I push both sticks forward and we fly through the glass and into the building. The glow from my engines shows desks and chairs and rows of cubicles, all of them immediately crushed under the Ax. A few things catch fire from our passing.

"Are they following?"

Peter checks. "Too much debris to tell, but probably!"

We crash through the far end of the building and I pull up, cutting hard to the left and then swooping back down toward the street. A quick check of the map shows I've confused them briefly, which I hope is enough for my next plan. It has to be enough.

I point at the live map. "I need you to figure out how to shut off the transponder or whatever it is that's letting them know where we are."

"On it," Peter says, and begins fiddling with the controls.

I bring the Ax down low over the avenue, then dive down another side street. Then it's up another avenue till the next block. Constant zigging and zagging. I can't risk being in their line of sight again.

Peter seems to figure it out right away, erasing our dot from the map.

"How did you know how to do that?"

He shrugs and says, "Luck. I hope this is one of your better ideas."

"Me too," I say.

On the map an Ax is nearing the corner ahead, trying to cut us off, so I make a hard right up the next avenue, staying low, but really leaning on the throttle. The four engines whine louder, glowing brighter, and we rocket forward, block after block. Just as the Ax behind us is about to come into view, I swing down another side street, almost clipping the top of an abandoned semitruck.

From there it's just a little bit farther until I'm on the West Side Highway, headed north above cars skewed all over the road. The gun turrets left behind by True Earth are still in the middle of the road amid scattered vehicles, but they're dark now. No more attacks are coming across the river, at least from anything that runs on electricity. And with no way to communicate, any kind of ground assault from the outside will be slow in arriving.

"I think you lost them," Peter says, eyes on the map. That doesn't make me get off the throttle. The buildings are a blur to the right. Soon we're at the north end of the island.

"There could be a second hidden transponder," Peter says. "We should land a good bit away in case they can still find us."

I swing off the highway and land just southeast of the George Washington Bridge. Once I'm on the ground, I kill the engines immediately (which seem to die gratefully, sputtering out with a four-note death rattle), open the canopy, and scan the area. Any civilians who saw us land could quickly gather a mob and force us to defend ourselves. But the coast seems clear.

We hop out. Peter carries the last RAW on his back. The Ax itself looks like it's been through a meat grinder.

A few blocks north we hit 181st Street. The Washington Heights neighborhood is much less dense than the downtown area, filled with smaller apartment buildings all the same color—a dingy, brownish brick. Fires burn in the streets, most of them cars. Unlike other parts of the city, people are actually outside here. It doesn't have the sense of panic I anticipated. One of the little farmer's markets is still open, lit by torches and guarded by armed men. I look closer and see it's actually a dozen or so cops in police riot gear. There's a line of people waiting for their share of food. The sight of order being maintained isn't enough to give me hope, but it's good to see.

We continue traveling north toward Kellogg's apartment building, secure in our disguises. A man starts following us, but then he sees the RAW I'm holding and decides he's actually going the wrong way.

"Alone at last," Peter says, and we both stop at the same time, facing each other in the dark. He kisses me then, hard and fast, and the RAW gets caught between us, pinching my injured hand, but I don't care. I kiss him back just as hard. I sling an arm around his neck, and his hand presses on the small of my back, pulling us together so there isn't an inch of space.

I think about the promise I made before killing the eyeless. We were in the showers of our old school, just a door between us, and I promised we would talk when everything was over. The promise was a lie, and I knew it at the time. But here I am, getting a second chance I don't deserve.

I want to fulfill my promise this time.

"I like kissing you," he says.

"Then do it."

He tilts his head to the side, just slightly, and I can see the barest outline of his smile in the darkness. Then he kisses me again.

"I want to stop fighting," I say against his lips.

"We will soon. Just a little bit longer. We just have to fight a little bit longer."

I know there's still so much to do, so many answers to find, so much that's uncertain. But I listen to him anyway, and we keep walking. We hold hands. And for five seconds, I think everything might turn out all right. But those five seconds can't stand up to the black hole I feel inside me.

We pass a wine store, which I know is empty before I can see inside. I imagine people inside their bitter-cold apartments drinking themselves to death, or drinking just to keep warm. On the side of the store is a colorful mural of cartoon stick figures crossing a street, with the words *ALL YOU NEED IS LOVE* above them in big poofy letters. If only ...

When we reach Kellogg's building, there's a man in the lobby to greet us.

With a shotgun.

He levels it at us. We hold the RAWs loosely, barrels angled toward the floor.

"We're here to meet Kellogg," I say. "He sent us. He's on his way."

"The soldier man?" the guy says. He's wearing a blue pea-coat, hipsterish glasses with big black frames, and a nice, stylish scarf. It's weird to see him with the shotgun in his hands. Like with Natalie, the end of the barrel bobs and sways. Some people should not carry weapons.

"Please don't accidentally shoot us," Peter says. "Notice how we came in? Nice and easy? We're on your side."

"Oh really?" the man says.

"What apartment is Kellogg's?" I say.

"I don't know. 2H or 2G or something."

"May we go there?" I step forward slowly, curl my fingers around the top of the barrel slowly, and then push it toward the floor, also slowly. The man's lower lip is quivering.

"They put me on guard duty for the next hour," the man says. I'm not sure if that's a yes or a no.

"What if we just stay here with you?" I say. "We can wait for Kellogg." At least we're out of the wind.

He nods after a moment. "That sounds fine, I guess." And then he says, "My wife died."

"I'm really sorry," I say, because I don't know what else to say.

"I was out looking for food and someone broke into our apartment. Next week I was going to start buying more groceries and stop getting so much takeout. We had talked about it. About how much money we were wasting on delivery, you know."

I nod like I know what he's talking about. Is there even a way to make someone feel better in this situation? Probably not. Not with faces like mine and Peter's.

"They left her tangled in the bathroom, half-wrapped in the shower curtain."

"I'm sorry," I say again.

"But one of them dropped his wallet. I knew who he was." He hefts the shotgun, as if that explains everything, and in a way it does.

No one speaks again. We settle onto the floor facing the door with our weapons across our laps. Peter rests his head against my shoulder, and then I rest my head on his. Somehow his hair still smells good. I wonder what he would do if he came home and found me dead on the bathroom floor. I actually feel bad for the imaginary people who kill me.

After what feels like hours, Kellogg shows up with around a hundred people in tow.

Kellogg shakes the man's hand. "Zachary," he says. I never thought to ask for the man's name.

"Who are all these people?" Zachary says, clearly not happy to see them.

"Survivors. Including most of my men."

"We can't feed them. The building has enough food for a few days. And that's with weak rations. You get that, right?"

"I do. We'll think of something."

"You gonna raid another building with your soldiers and their guns?" His eyes fill with tears; he's thinking of his wife, no doubt.

Kellogg holds his gaze. "No. I'm not. I said we'll think of something." He wedges the door to the lobby open with a newspaper, and people begin to file inside. One of his soldiers comes in, and Kellogg says, "Make a fire in the courtyard. It'll be hidden there."

"These people are hungry," the soldier says.

"It's been four days. They don't know what hungry is yet."

Then Noble and Sophia stagger in with the rest of the

crowd. They manage a smile for me and Peter, and I hug them both at the same time.

"Safe trip?" Noble says.

"There have been worse," I reply. "You?"

"Spiders," Sophia says, shivering from either the cold or the word. "We burned through a lot of ammunition, but there were only two casualties."

That night we gather around a fire in the courtyard, which is taller than anyone. People clump around it, no one talking much. A few people complain about being hungry. The harsh firelight coupled with the darkness just beyond it hide Peter's and my faces well. People that do recognize us give us dirty looks, but I assume Kellogg briefed them all on who we are and why we're here.

As the night goes on it's actually not that bad of a time. One guy starts telling rude jokes, and people laugh. I see two kids playing with little toy cars, packing the snow into makeshift ramps.

Then I see Albin standing next to the fire. I gasp, but he holds a finger to his lips. I look at the faces around him, but no one is looking at him. He's hidden himself in their minds.

"Meet me in the park," he says. "Come alone, or everyone dies."

I blink and he disappears.

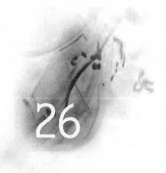

26

I try not to look startled, but Peter must notice something change on my face. "What is it?" he says.

I just shake my head. "Uh..."

I stand up, shaking the stiffness from my cold joints. I stretch my hands over my head, trying to seem casual, but my eyes are searching for Albin in all the shadows, even though I know I won't find him.

"Where are you going?" Peter says.

"Do you trust me?"

"Yes." The look on his face says no.

"If I'm not back in fifteen minutes, get everyone out."

"Miranda, what is it?"

He tries to stand up, but I press my hand to his shoulder. "Trust me."

"Okay, but don't go far."

"Not far," I say.

I leave the light of the fire and feel my way back inside to the chilly hallway. People have lit candles to line the hallway, which is thoughtful, but they're using too many. If we fail, people will wish they'd been more careful with how many they burned.

The guards at the main door look at me questioningly.

"Kellogg wants me to do a patrol," I say, which is good enough for them.

I step into the cold again, then unsling the RAW from my back. The few people on the street give me a wide berth. A man taking his dog for a walk nods at me, and I hold up a hand and say, "I'm not one of them." He just hurries away with his dog.

Three men on the other side of the street group up behind a UPS truck, and I can hear them muttering and pointing. I break into a run, ignoring the stinging cold air in my lungs. The three men are pursuing, but halfheartedly. The street ends at a traffic circle with a bunch of leafless trees planted in the middle. I skirt around it and see the entrance to the park straight ahead.

And standing right there is a man wearing a suit of

plum-colored armor. Albin holds my gaze for a moment, then turns around and runs into the park.

"Oh come *on*," I say. We can't just talk out here? I have to follow him inside?

The cautious part of me thinks it could be a trap, but the sensible part knows that's not logical. If True Earth knew where we were, they could just hover an Ax over the courtyard and drop a bomb on us. Plus Albin only called for me, when Peter is just as valuable. No, this is something else.

I jog after him, eyes scanning left and right for any movement. I level my RAW at a black squirrel climbing a tree, then spin again as a few dead leaves rustle over a mound of snow. Somehow it's lighter here—unnaturally light. I can see the trees all around me, their bare branches swaying back and forth.

It's an illusion. Albin is letting me see so I can follow him. Above, the sky is still pure black, a night sky without stars or a moon.

I move deeper into the park. Behind me, the wall of darkness is steadily filling in again, a black sheet pushing me onward.

"This is far enough," I say.

No it isn't, Albin says in my head.

I hear the sound of rushing wind, and behind me the wall of darkness moves faster than before. I break into a run, up a set of stairs and into an open area set against a cliff overlooking the Hudson River. I sprint across the stones covering the ground, but then something invisible and solid strikes me mid-thigh. I topple over sideways. My hands slam down, grabbing at whatever tripped me. They catch on something in the air, what feels like a rock wall, and then my feet are dangling over nothing. The RAW is gone.

The darkness dissolves back into light, with Albin hovering above me as I dangle over the side of a cliff.

It's so obvious now I could laugh—or cry. Instead I only glare up at him. He tricked me with an illusion once again. I thought I was far away from the edge, but I wasn't. The rock wall that looked ten feet away was right in front of me.

Albin smiles down at me with that perfect smile—perfect in structure, at least, since the smile doesn't feel all that genuine. But his honey-colored eyes are warm, as before.

"You realize I'm doing this for my protection only," he says. "That weapon was too dangerous for you to have if we're going to talk."

"I needed it, you idiot. You have more. And I don't trust you."

"Then we have something in common already."

He takes a laborious breath, then looks around our little clearing high above the river.

"If I help you up, can I trust you?" he says.

"I came all this way, didn't I? Alone."

"A simple yes or no will suffice."

"Let's call it a truce instead."

He grabs my wrist and hauls me up with considerable strength. I swing my legs back onto solid ground.

We stand a safe distance away from each other. "You're strong," he says.

"Thanks."

"Which is why I came to you. The girl who has been through so much. Through multiple lives already. I know what you are willing to risk."

My cheek tingles when I think about the bruise he gave me. "Your illness is gone," I say.

He sniffles, like a reflex, and then coughs on leftover gunk in his lungs. "I'm recovering. I come from a world without disease. It is to my shame that I wasn't ready to experience this place."

"What are you, some kind of robot?"

He actually laughs. "No. Well, parts of me are not biological, but I assure you, I am almost completely organic. I come from a world separate from your time line entirely, or rather, one which split away long ago. You could call my world a rival of True Earth's, both societies trying to prove how utterly *perfect* they are."

"But you work together...."

"Not exactly. One of the leaders of my world liked what

the director of True Earth was doing, and he tried to help. Walk with me."

He starts toward the other end of the open area, but I don't move.

"How can I trust anything you're saying?" I call after him.

He spins around, brow lowered in anger. "Don't you see? You're only here because of me. Do you think the director was really going to let you go, only to allow you to keep fighting back? I hid your meeting with Olivia from her, giving you time to escape. The director was disappointed and surprised when you didn't show up in the Verge. But now she's moved on to anger."

"Why the change of heart in helping me?" If I can trust him, I do need his help. But I will never forget the hand he had in Rhys's death. I can't.

"Because the director lied to me, and to my people. I came here because I thought we were destroying your world completely. I thought this was another errant world that might one day be a threat to all others. Then I discover that, no, it's the past of True Earth, and they have no intention of destroying it. When I discovered the lie, I reported it and was ordered to stop the director. My goals are now in line with yours. We only serve True Earth when it serves *us*."

This should be good news, but instead it churns my stomach. What evil logic. "It's that simple, huh? You had no problem destroying us before, but now that you know hurting us is helping True Earth, you're against it."

"Essentially," he says. "At the start of this mission we thought there could be peace between us, but as the name implies, there is only one true earth. The director lied because she wanted our Key, which we loaned to her, against our good judgment. And then she lost it to one of her creations, this East person. Now we don't want her to have it at all."

I start walking with him. I make the choice to trust him. We follow a trail down a hill side by side.

"You're cold," he says with kindness that sounds a little too false. Almost like he's trying it out.

"I'm fine."

But then I blink, and the barren ice world that is New York transforms into a summer day. The trees have leaves, there is a gentle breeze, and birds chirp all around us. I can smell flowers and new grass. And the air on my face feels warm. It almost doesn't matter that it's not real.

"How do you do that?"

"My world has created warriors, not unlike the Roses of True Earth. But we try not to terrify our enemies into submission."

"Just deceive."

He nods. No way he can deny it. Then we come across our first body, a middle-aged man on his stomach, frozen and

244

thick with frost. It looks so out of place in the illusion. Albin doesn't bother to hide it.

"So this Key leads to a room...."

He nods again. "We created a room from where the Black can be controlled. Where it can be used as a weapon."

"If you're so powerful you can dupe the director, why don't you just take it?"

"I have to follow rules about interference. There are other worlds watching, all the time. The multiverse is bigger than you can imagine, with nearly infinite time lines."

"What do you want me to do once I have the Key?"

"There's only one thing you can do, isn't there? If you remove the Black from this world, power will be restored, and it will recover. But once the Black is released the way it has been, it can't go back. It's out there and must occupy another world. Imagine puncturing a can of soda and trying to put the liquid back inside. It wouldn't work."

"So it has to go somewhere. Where?"

He stops walking. So do I. "You know where it has to go," he says.

True Earth.

He picks a flower growing next to his foot and holds it up between us, inspecting it.

My throat is tight. I swallow, and it gets even tighter. "So you expect me to just destroy their world. *Our* future."

"I'm afraid at this juncture, you can either live in eternal darkness now or eternal darkness later. It seems like a problem I'd rather deal with in a thousand years, wouldn't you say? And who knows. Perhaps in a thousand years, your world will figure out a solution before it happens."

He lets the flower fall, and it disappears before it hits the ground. As does the rest of the illusion. The cold hits me all at once, and I start shivering despite my armor and clothes.

"I think deep down you know that's been the choice all along. What are you willing to do, how *terrible* are you willing to become, in order to save your world?"

My teeth are chattering. "You don't care about us. We're nothing to you. We're just animals."

"That's true. But I see that you're not nothing to one another. Perspective is everything."

"Why do I think you're just too afraid to do it yourself?"

"I don't know," he says.

We're back on the road to Kellogg's building, where I will really have to make the choice.

"Even if I got the Key and do what you want—and I'm not saying I will—what guarantee do I have that some other True Earth won't spring up and become a threat to us again? Or even *your* world, which I know nothing about, by the way."

He's silent for a long moment.

"The Dark Room"—he says it like that, *The Dark Room*—"doesn't just direct the flow of the Black...."

"Tell me."

"From the Dark Room, a person could poison the Black forever. They could make it so no one could ever travel through it and survive ever again."

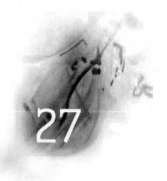

27

"Would you really let me do that?"

He nods. "I would."

The idea is too perfect. To finally be left alone, to just exist the way we're supposed to. If we destroy ourselves in time, that's on us. It's a huge choice, but is it the right one?

Albin must sense my hesitation. "Listen. Only so much Black has been added to your world. You can transfer that amount back. It will not destroy True Earth, but it will plunge them into the same darkness. You will be sentencing many to die, but many will live."

"Why can't I just release it into an empty world? Some place they've already destroyed? I don't want to wreck our future—*I can't.*"

"The Black can only be returned to its source. Adding the Black to a different universe would be another process entirely and would have no effect on your world. You would just be ruining someone else's day."

"But the director said she was going to remove the Black in a few weeks. . . . Surely she wouldn't have been turning it back on herself."

"Then maybe she was planning to send it further into the future. It must remain in your shared world, at one time or another."

He looks me in the eyes. I stop walking. "I am telling the truth when I say I don't care about your future. As long as it's no threat to my world again, the condition of it matters to me not at all. This is not about vengeance. It's practical. It's a blameless way to end a threat with an infinite number of universes watching."

Somehow, I believe him. It horrifies me, but I understand him.

"Then if I poison the Black, and traveling through it is no longer possible, I will lock in the future. There will be no way to tamper with it ever again." I'm talking to myself now.

"Yes." Albin sighs. "Are you going to do this or not? Because if not, I have to find another Miranda."

"Why another Miranda?"

"Only the director has the clearance to enter the Dark

Room. And you are the same person. No other clone could do this."

"I feel so special."

A moment passes before Albin says, "You won't when the time comes."

Before turning the corner and being in the line of sight of Kellogg's building, Albin stops. "I will be with you going forward, but I will hide myself from the eyes of everyone else. Only you will be able to see me."

"What do you want me to do?"

"Use your brain, you poor, unevolved creature. What do you think?"

"You want me to bring my team along."

"I want you to bring everyone along. Everyone who will come. This is your one chance. If you're injured, you need others who will pick up the slack."

We go back inside, past the two men guarding the door.

"Where is your gun?" the left one says. Sharp guy.

"Hidden," I say without thinking. Not sure why I would hide it out there.

The men share a look, but I just walk into the lobby.

Down the hallway Peter is walking ahead of Noble, shrugging off his hand. "I'm going after—" Peter freezes when he sees me, and his jaw tightens.

"I wanted to stretch my legs," I say quickly. "Patrol a little."

"Don't lie to me."

I march toward him and grab his hand. Noble is staring at me, waiting.

"I have news."

"Well, let's hear it," Peter says.

"Not here. Get Sophia."

In Kellogg's apartment I brief them all, including Kellogg. Noble is instantly wary.

But before he can ask a question, Kellogg does. "Where is this *Albin* person right now?"

"Um . . . outside the door."

"You led him *here*?" Kellogg grabs his rifle off the table. I snatch it out of his hands.

"Haven't you been listening? He knew we were here and yet we're still alive. He's giving us a way to save the people of this planet. The *only* way, unless you have a better idea," I challenge him. "Last I heard, nobody had a solid plan. So we're doing this."

Kellogg tries to stare me down, but I'm not the kind of person it would work on. Finally he sighs. "I guess you should introduce us, then."

"Albin, come in," I say. The door opens and Albin stands in the frame. Everyone can see him now.

"Greetings," he says.

Sophia is the only one to respond. "Hi."

"My men are ready to fight and die," Kellogg says. "But I have to make sure it's for a good reason. It has to count toward something."

"Time is short," Albin says. "People are dying every second. So here is what we must do."

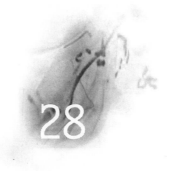

28

The plan is pretty simple. We storm the Verge, and I try to get to East and therefore possess the Key. Albin says East will be as close to the Black as he can be, which makes sense, I guess. So he'll be under the Verge, or as close to under it as possible. The last time I was under a Verge, I was about to blow myself up. Good memories.

Albin will hide me for as long as he can, but we'll have to be fast.

I leave my outer clothing in Kellogg's apartment; I don't need to hide anymore. Five minutes later I'm standing in the courtyard in front of the survivors who came with us. They gave me a milk crate to stand on, so their heads are tilted up slightly. The fire casts black shadows over their eyes, giving them a demonic appearance. I can pick out Kellogg's men wearing their urban camouflage; there are fewer than I remember.

"So..."

A great beginning. Someone coughs. Two of the kids already look bored, and one is surreptitiously making a snowball.

I take a breath. *You've done harder things than this.*

"We have a plan to end this. I know many of you still have no idea what's going on, but you know what the damage has been. My friends and I have a plan to stop this. To make everything the way it was."

"So *do* it," one woman holding a tiny, shivering dog says. I try not to glare at her.

"What I need is help."

I wait for someone to say *Help how?* but no one does.

"I need as many people as possible to come back to Central Park with us. You'll get a weapon, and the soldiers here will instruct you how to use it. I have a way of sneaking into the Verge undetected, but it's important we draw the Roses—the enemies—out and occupy their attention."

"Why?" the woman with the dog asks. I hate her and I hate her dog.

"I'm not sure how long our mission will take once we're inside. Or what kind of alarms will be tripped. So I need you

254

to make some noise, to provide the best distraction you can, and then ... run. You can use the subway tunnels to come back here. If we succeed, you'll be able to return to your homes. If we don't, then this is it. For the rest of your lives, this is it."

I guess I should say more, but I don't know what.

That guy coughs again.

"Take five minutes to think about it. If you're in, talk to one of Kellogg's men." Just because they escaped with Kellogg doesn't guarantee they'll want to fight when the time comes. I just have to hope for the best.

I find Peter's face in the crowd, and he gives me a thumbs-up and a wink.

"Thanks," I say, then step off the milk crate. Someone actually claps. Then someone else claps. It doesn't catch, but it is funny. I guess if this were a movie, everyone would do a battle cry or something.

Peter and Sophia walk with me back to Kellogg's apartment, where he has a last-minute spread on the table. There's a half-eaten tub of hummus, some tomato juice, some eggs. Kellogg is cooking with Sterno. "I figure we should use this stuff now. Since we're either coming back heroes or not coming back at all. Please, eat. You'll need the energy." He notices Albin standing off to the side. "Do you eat?"

"I eat," Albin says.

"Then have at it."

Albin looks startled, like he didn't expect kindness. I didn't, either. But he seems warmed by it.

We eat our fill, and I notice my hands are shaking. Peter does too. He takes my right one and holds it in his lap, squeezing it gently.

"Are you sure you want to do this?" he asks.

"Of course not." Though I seem to remember already committing. I can't imagine just sitting by and accepting this as our new reality. I won't.

"Actually," I say, "I am sure."

He leans in and drops his voice to a whisper. His eyes look almost black in the candlelight. "Then I'm with you." He kisses where my cheek meets my ear.

Peter turns to Albin. "How are you keeping the director unaware of all this? Especially with how far away we are right now?"

"I'm not. I assisted in your escape, nothing more. The director is searching for you now. . . . And if she catches you, she won't be as liberal with the freedom she gives you as she was before."

The door opens behind us. One of Kellogg's men enters holding a SCAR—a Special Operations Forces Combat Assault Rifle. Very powerful by earth standards, but nowhere near the RAW. Not even in the same universe, so to speak.

"We're ready," the soldier says.

✾　✾　✾

There's a brief argument to catch a few hours of sleep first, but that's quickly shot down. There is too little time. In the next day, more people without water will die. In the end we have twenty-seven volunteers, men and women of all ages, plus the fifteen soldiers under Kellogg's command. Kellogg has to tell a nine-year-old girl that she can't come.

As we're walking back to the nearest subway station, Kellogg hands me a small black pouch. Inside is a knife. "US Navy MK3. Used by Navy Seals across the globe. Best for silent kills." I suddenly miss Beacon, my sword, very much. This knife is a decent size, straight and black, no glare—not that there's a chance of glare with the constant darkness. One side is serrated in case I need to saw through rope or build a log cabin or something.

"Thanks," I say, slinging the pouch around my waist. I stick the memory shot Noble gave me inside as well.

"That belonged to my friend," he says.

"I'll take good care of it."

We take the subway tunnels back to Central Park, led by my team with our RAWs held in the ready position. Any spiders we come across will be quickly demolished, but all we find are the corpses from the first trip. Dead arms among the tracks, most of them being nibbled on by rats, which don't bother scattering at our approach. The creatures even died like spiders, on their backsides, arms curled inward, palms up.

Flashlights aren't working, so Kellogg's men form up around us carrying road flares. I ask Albin to assist, but he wants to rest his mind for what's ahead. One brave soldier walks about ten meters in front of us to make sure we're not walking into a trap.

The first few miles are easy enough. We just follow the rails—how hard can that be? But people are getting tired, many of them having just made the journey in the other direction. It can't be more than one hundred and thirty blocks. Twenty blocks is supposed to be a mile in New York, so that's less than seven miles. Crybabies. Though I should be grateful any of them came along. I *am* grateful.

Sophia works her way to my side at some point. She nudges me with her elbow.

"What's up?"

"Sorry," she says. "I want to say sorry. I've been unkind."

"We've all been under serious stress." It seems like the thing to say.

"That's no excuse. You're the closest thing I've ever had to a sister. I've never had anyone besides Noble, not since I was too young to remember."

That makes me feel terrible. If I'm her sister, I haven't been a very good one. I haven't bothered to get to know her at all, or comfort her after Rhys's death. I wish Olive, *my* Olive, were still here; she would be a better friend to Sophia.

"I was angry," she continues.

"About Rhys."

"Yes. And I'm sure you were too."

"I still am. That's why we're doing this. He died so we'd have a chance to keep fighting."

She nods, her dark skin glowing orange in the torchlight. "Yes he did."

We walk for another hundred feet.

"When this is over, let's go do something normal together," she says.

"Okay. What do normal people do?"

"I guess we'll find out. Oh! We could go to the Metropolitan Museum of Art. The Met. Have you heard of it?"

"I have."

"Noble took me and Rhys there and showed us the different exhibits. The man seems to know everything about everything. It was so amazing to see the history of your world in art. Noble would sometimes point at something especially beautiful and say, *This is what we're fighting for*, or something like that."

"That sounds like him," I say, and up ahead he looks over his shoulder and smiles at us.

Sophia lets out a big, satisfied sigh. "That was a great day. Then we ate lunch from a cart on the street. Like the ones back where I come from, but the food wasn't made of dead rats."

"You know, I've never eaten from a food cart."

"That's what we'll do, then!" Sophia says. "The museum and a food cart."

"It sounds wonderful." Too wonderful to think about for more than a few seconds without feeling tired.

It takes a couple hours to get back to Central Park, since we stop several times for breaks. Kellogg says it'll all be for nothing if people can't sprint once they have True Earth's attention. There isn't much talking, so we can hear sounds traveling up and down the tunnels. A distant, ghostly shout. Water dripping somewhere. The scuttling sounds of spiders, which are really just echoes from our dragging footsteps.

And then we come out of the tunnels, a safe distance to the north of the Verge, out into the same darkness. We walk to the edge of the park, where we can barely see the outline of the Verge. Some of the surrounding fires have died, and there's even less light for it to reflect now.

Peter steps over to Albin. "I want to go in with her."

Albin shakes his head. "I'm getting fatigued. I won't be able to hide you both from everyone."

"I didn't ask," Peter says.

Albin just looks at me, eyebrows raised like, *Is this guy serious?*

"No unnecessary risks," I say to both of them. Peter looks away to hide his anger.

I try my best to address the group, though I can't see many of them in the gloom. "If the flying machines show up, let them chase you into the trees. Move east or west from there, and scatter as best you can. Hole up. If you can make it back up to Washington Heights, great. We'll know if this is over soon enough." The plan is to make as much noise as possible to draw out the Roses, but the strategy once we have their attention is little more than *run*.

Kellogg appears on my right. "Are you ready?"

"As ready as . . . you know."

He grimaces, nodding. "Sadly, I do. I'll remain near the Verge with your teammates, just to the north. If things go badly, we're all going in after you."

Albin steps up. "If it's impossible to get to East ourselves, we'll come find you."

"Roger that." Kellogg whistles softly at his men and starts away, leading the group of citizen fighters.

Peter puts his hand on my shoulder. "You don't have to do this. I can go."

"No," is all I say.

"Dammit, Miranda, you don't always have to be the one."

"This is the last time."

I'm about to lean in to kiss him, but he turns away, muttering something I don't hear. It feels like I've been slapped. I could die in the next five minutes—we could *all* die, and he's doing this now? Does he think we have such a small chance?

Then it's Noble's turn to say good-bye. "You know what to do. I have complete faith in you." He kisses me on the cheek.

The groups move in their respective directions, disappearing fast into the dark. Soon Albin and I are the only ones left.

"You've been fighting for a long time," he says. It's not a question.

"I have."

"Do you have one more in you?"

29

I have to use my knife sooner than expected. The distraction has already begun—people screaming, firing guns into the sky—and it's working. Thirty seconds ago, an alarm sounded and a dozen Roses armed with RAWs and straight swords descended from different levels of the Verge and entered the freezing night. But two Roses remained behind to block the entrance. I made quick work of their throats, wondering what it must be like to be standing still one second, then have an invisible force spill your blood in the next. Albin and I move the bodies inside, but there's nowhere to hide them or the blood smeared all over the floor.

As we step inside the Verge, I'm startled to see the Black is gone, replaced with a solid metal floor.

"Where is it?" I say, but then I remember how the Black was below the floor in Gane's Verge.

"The director had the portal moved once all the Axes and Thorns came through. Just an added layer of security."

A rectangular hole is cut into the floor. Inside it, a staircase curls down and to the left. We take the staircase, coming across two more sentries as we descend, both of them Mirandas. I break their necks swiftly, trying to avoid more bloodshed. I feel cold while I do it, but not as cold as Rhys must have felt facedown in the snow when the sword pierced his back.

The steps end abruptly at a door. "Am I hidden?" I ask. Our breath is echoing down here. I can't hear any other sounds from above, no gunfire, nothing. I hope the others are safe.

"You will be, once I see if there is anyone to hide you from."

"Can you feel them through the door?"

"Yes. Right now the only one I feel is East."

"No guards?"

"We've gotten this far. You have to trust me."

I do trust him, strangely, so I open the door to find a circular chamber ringed in a catwalk with an X in the middle. In the very middle of the X, in the very middle of the chamber, is East, bound in chains on his knees, almost exactly like he was in the bathroom at Penn Station. Beneath the catwalk is the Black, a pulsating eye I'm careful not to look at.

East lifts his head slowly at the sound of the opening door.

"We've met before," I call to him. "I'm a friend."

He nods, like he knew this all along. "Alpha team, the second one at least. Yes."

"How did you know?"

"Your left hand is injured."

I hold my hand up as if confirming. It tingles. My last two fingers are curled awkwardly, making it obvious my hand isn't 100 percent.

I walk toward him, trying to ignore the limitless void beneath my feet.

"Come to free me?" he says. He lifts up his chains. I have no idea how to get them off. Would my RAW help, or would the kinetic energy just transfer to him and blow his arm off?

"Yes, but first I need your help with something." I look behind me; Albin is still standing in the doorway, but I can tell East hasn't seen him.

"To enter the Dark Room," he says.

"Yes."

"To destroy True Earth."

"At least partially."

"That's a lot of responsibility for a young woman."

"They've left me no choice."

He nods. "True. They didn't give me a choice, either. Some things you are born into." He considers this, then laughs dryly. "Maybe *born* isn't the right word."

"You had a choice. You left the creators, like Noble did."

He nods again. "That's true." I can't get over that this is the man Noah would've grown up to be. This is him as an adult. He would've been just as handsome. With eyes just as dark. "Some of us see more clearly than others," he says.

I kneel at his chains, inspecting them for some kind of weakness, even though I know there will be none. The chains are solid. I'd have to cut his arm off with the Navy SEAL knife, which he would probably object to.

"No offense, but I didn't think it would be you standing here," he says. "The director fighting back against herself. Interesting."

"We're nothing alike."

"Yes. I hope you keep it that way."

"I'm not worried." Much.

"You know, you'd probably be doing True Earth a favor—or rather us a favor—by eliminating them as a possible future," he goes on. "I've spent several years there on and off. They don't fight the way we do. To them, nuclear weapons are the equivalent of throwing stones."

My mind can't even imagine what that means.

"Have you been to the Dark Room?" I ask.

"I have, but they blindfolded me and covered my ears too. They only needed me to get inside, then they did the rest. I have no details that could help you."

"I have a way to reverse the Black, then to poison it, to make sure no one travels through it again."

"Good!"

I've given what I must do a lot of thought. It may be the only option, but I will still be *killing people*. I will become a mass murderer of people who never asked for a war.

"I was hoping you would do it," I say quietly.

"I'm sure you were. But though I think it's necessary, I don't know if I am capable of following through."

That stops me cold. If East isn't capable, am I? Once my finger is on the trigger, will I pull it? Even right now, standing here, I can't know for sure. I've done what's necessary before, but this is different.

"I know what you mean," I say.

"Miranda. Stay strong. Let's worry about getting these chains off first." His eyes drift to the tip of the RAW poking above my left shoulder. "That gun should do it."

"I thought of that...but I'm afraid it might actually kill you."

He shrugs. "Got a better idea?"

He's right. "You sound a lot like him, you know."

"Who?"

"Noah. My Noah. I loved him. He was a good friend."

East actually smiles. "Of course he was. If he was me."

I aim the RAW at where his chains are bolted to the

catwalk, thumbing the power dial down to one. Then I step back far enough in case it blows a hole through the floor.

I'm about to fire when I hear a familiar sound. It's the sound of a paint can getting kicked over. The sound of liquid splashing over a hard surface. It can only be one thing.

30

I whirl around, prepared to fire, because I know what I'm
going to see.

It's Nina, holding Albin up by the neck with one hand.
He's limp like a rag doll, blood running down the scales on
the front of his suit.

I aim the RAW at her, but she snaps her free wrist and the
lights flicker, and the RAW powers down in my hands. I drop
it on the deck. The armor she wears shimmers weirdly, like
it's surrounded by a thin force field that hovers a millimeter
off her body.

She lets Albin fall to the floor. "Did you really think you'd
get away with it?"

She pulls a RAW off her back.

"If you shoot," I say, "you could kill East. I don't think your mother would be too happy about that."

"No, I wouldn't," a voice says behind me. I whirl again. The director's standing at the other end of the catwalk, behind East. A door is open behind her. Two ways out, two ways in, both guarded by the most dangerous people I've ever met.

"A valiant attempt, Miranda," the director says. "But we've known everything all along. You escaped because I *let you* escape. You've been supervised this whole time."

By who?

Olivia steps through the doorway behind the director, and it's like a hammer strike to the chest. No, it can't be her. She hasn't been with us. Her face is carefully blank.

"I thought we had an understanding," the director continues. "I can't tell you how sad this makes me." And she does seem sad, genuinely. "I thought you wanted to make this world a better place, not abandon it to fight a pointless battle."

"Let me do it," Nina says behind me. "Let's create a new future."

The director ignores her. "Olivia, would you please free the man chained to the floor? I think it's time we visit the Dark Room again."

Olivia walks past the director to East, but something is off—she looks frightened. She's not in control. I'm frozen, watching, waiting to see what happens next. My mind is racing, but I can't focus on anything without thinking of the people fighting above me. If the director knew I was here, if she knew Albin was helping me, were they expecting the assault? Did I send them all into a trap?

Olivia kneels next to East and begins working on the chains around his wrists. She unlocks the right one with a big brass key and is about to do the other when the director moves. I don't even have time to cry out. In an instant the director snatches up the chain, whips it around Olivia's throat, and lifts her off her feet. The other end of the chain is still anchored to the floor, giving her leverage. The key clatters to the catwalk, an inch from the edge.

I rush forward, screaming, but Nina grabs me from behind. I try to spin in her grasp, frantic now as the director chokes the life out of Olivia, but Nina is impossibly strong, much stronger than the one I fought before. She's trying to throw me into the Black, but I keep my feet planted, stretching out for Olivia, who is only inches away, her eyes red with burst capillaries. The director is grinning. She drops Olivia to the deck, and Olivia doesn't move. Meanwhile, East has been working on his left wrist with the key—he's almost free, but it's too late. The director is coming at me, her face flushed with exertion and rage.

It all happens so fast.

East hits her from behind with a chain.

She whirls on him, cocking her fist back.

I lunge for her and release the ever-present tension in my brain. I let it go completely this time; pain and relief wash over me as my fear waves spread out. Nina's grip on me weakens just enough to allow me to grab the director, but Nina is on my back the next second, and soon all four of us are jammed together, grabbing, elbowing, kneeing, moving. . . .

East swings his chain at us, and we stumble, hands grabbing at limbs. The chain cracks the director above her ear. My foot slips off the side of the catwalk, and then we're all dropping toward the mouth of hell. The director's head whips around, blood flying from a cut on her temple, and I catch a glimpse of her wide eyes, the most honest expression I've ever seen her make. And then we hit the dark.

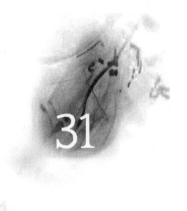

31

I open my eyes.

We're in a small room. One wall is made of the Black, while the other three are white. In the middle is a desk with an old computer on it, complete with a big, bulky monitor. East and Nina are struggling on the other side of the desk, and the director is on her hands and knees, facing away from me, blood dripping from the wound on her head. She's dazed; now is the time to finish her. I stand up as East gets his chain around Nina's neck. My head is swimming with heat, and I'm reminded of Noble's warning—*Wait too long and you could burn out.* With shaking hands, I uncap the syringe he gave me and stick it into my neck. The cool liquid enters my bloodstream and spreads through my brain, and the simmering heat drops to lukewarm. Sweat still springs on my forehead; I'm unsteady on my feet. I drop the syringe as Nina makes choking sounds on the other side of the room.

"Help me," East says quietly, straining.

But I can't. The director is recovering, rising to her feet now as she takes deep, heaving breaths. She turns around. Blood is running off her chin. She leaps toward me, preparing to crush me with a devastating punch. Instinctively I dive forward, under it, but her fist comes down early, onto my back, slamming me to the floor. My breath explodes out of me, and she doesn't give me a moment to catch it, kicking me right in the ribs.

I slide toward the wall of Black, groaning and twisting onto my side, a flaring pain spreading through my ribs and up through my neck. She kicks me again, and I cry out, writhing away, cheek against the ice-cold floor.

Out of the corner of my eye, I see East still struggling with Nina and the chains, neither getting the upper hand.

The director hovers over me, sneering down with such hatred that I wonder what things have to happen in my life for me to end up like her. What do I have to see?

"I was hoping you'd be more like me at this point," she says. She draws back her leg....

"I am," I say.

In a flash I have Kellogg's knife in my hand. I drive it

through her shin with all the strength I have left. She howls, and I sweep her good leg out from under her before she can regain her balance. She slams down hard next to me, cracking her injured head on the floor. I spin around, then plant both feet on her back and shove her as hard as I can toward the wall made of Black. She slides right through and out of the room.

"Help," East says again as I stagger to my feet.

I'm trying to get around the desk when a wave of pain hits me, and I have to put both hands on the desk to hold myself up. The monitor is showing blocky green text. The agony in my head almost makes me throw up, but I swallow it down and push off toward East.

I'm too late. There's already blood on the floor. Nina holds a bloody knife in her hand, and she's trying to swing it around to stab East again. He can't stop her because he's got both hands on the chain, trying to choke the life out of her. I dive for her wrist and bend it until her fingers open and the knife drops in the blood. I hold her down and watch grimly as East finishes the job. Eventually she stops making noise, but he doesn't.

"Oh that hurts," he says. Blood is coming from under his left ribs. A lot of it. "Oh man."

"I'm sorry. I'm really sorry."

"Not your fault. She stuck me right away." He looks around the room. "Can you do this? Can you finish the job?"

I don't say anything. His eyes roll up into his head for a

second. He doesn't speak for a long time, but then he asks again, quieter, "Can you do this? Please?"

"I can."

"Say it with conviction. If you don't, everything was for nothing. And many will die."

"I *can*," I say again. "I can do it."

"I'm sorry you didn't choose this life," he says. "I'm sorry for my hand in it."

"It's okay." As I watch him bleed out, I see Noah in my mind, the blood running between his fingers in the lab at our old school. The very same blood spilled by the very same girl. What I would give to hear his voice inside my head again. To know that I wasn't alone.

He smiles. "No it's not." Then his eyes flutter and he rests his head on the floor, and I watch him take his last breath.

I stand up alone in the Dark Room.

I'm suddenly breathing very fast. I can't control it. The back of my neck feels cold and tingly. Here I am, in the place we've tried so hard to get to. And I'm just supposed to kill people. People I don't know. Innocent people. And yet if I don't, this darkness will remain.

Does that make it right? Or just necessary?

I walk around the desk and sit down in the chair. The monitor is on, the cursor blinking.

```
Black is currently holding in 8492
Do you want to:
Transfer Black
Move a new amount
Other options
```

I highlight `Transfer Black` and hit Enter.

```
Do you want to:
Transfer Black to source (5)
Transfer Black to new location (unavailable at
this time)
```

I highlight the only option.

```
Do you want to:
Add Black (will result in destruction of 5)
Transfer Only
```

Maybe in the future they're already expecting what I'm about to do. They could've prepared for it. Who knows. Who can imagine what the future looks like? As Albin said, we have a thousand years to figure it out.

If you do this, I tell myself, *you will truly start your path to becoming the director. This is how you become like her. This could be the first step.*

"I'm giving them the same chance they gave us," I say aloud.

I feel tears on my face. Can I really tap a few keys and have this result?

I have to.

I highlight Transfer Only. *Only,* it says. I'm only transferring. I'm only sending the Black back to where it came from. I look at the Enter key. It's just a key.

If I push the button, I will save the world.

If I push the button.

I will save the world.

I push the button.

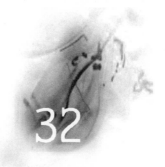

32

P rocessing...

Complete.

The screen goes back to the main menu. Just like that. Over. Done. I let out the breath I was holding.

Other options is highlighted now. The screen blurs from my tears, but I can't feel sorry or bad for myself. I made the choice.

I hit Enter.

Stop organics from entering Black (requires administrator password)

Stop synthetics from entering Black

Stop organics and synthetics from entering Black (requires administrator password)

I highlight the last option, which will encompass humans and machines. I don't want organics or synthetics entering the Black, ever.

I type the password at the prompt, the one Albin whispered in my ear: SOVEREIGN

```
Are you sure? The effects cannot be reversed.
Yes
No
```

It's one thing I am sure of. I enter `Yes`.

```
You have two minutes to leave this room.
```

The computer powers down, the soft fizz of electricity coming from inside the monitor fading away.

That's it. It's over. We're free. Until we have to deal with the inevitable future I've given us, that is. We have one thousand years.

We won. Yet it doesn't feel like a victory at all. I fall back in the chair like I've been struck, thinking about what I've done, and what it means.

Finally I stand up from the desk and look around the room. East's blood covers a quarter of it. Nina lies in a tangled heap. I'll never see her again, in any form. It's impossible.

We're free. We're free. But still, I sob against the desk, crying so hard I can't breathe. What happens now? I just go back home and do what? I won't even be able to see how True Earth fares in the coming days and weeks and months. I have no way of knowing if their life will go on uninterrupted, or if they're all going to die.

You had no choice. It was us or them.

I hope one day I can believe that. I hope one day I can remove the knife in my heart.

I stand up after some time has passed. I don't know how much. It could be one minute and fifty-seven seconds. Maybe deep down I want to get stuck here. Maybe it's what I deserve. But I guess I'm still human after all, because I grab East under the arms, then drag him to the Black and pass through it.

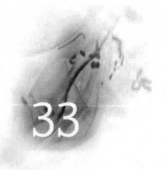

33

The director is on the platform when I return, on her knees and in custody, arms and legs bound in chains. Kellogg's men have guns on her from every angle. Her leg is still bleeding, dripping through the catwalk. She's so pale I don't know how she's still conscious.

Two soldiers grab East's body and heave him up and over the side of the catwalk.

I pull myself up, feeling returning to my legs as they escape the Black. Just as my legs break the surface completely, smoke begins to swirl underneath the director. I look closer. Each droplet of blood that hits the Black sizzles before bursting into a puff of midnight smoke. It's poisoned, just like Albin said.

I made it back to my world just in time. I almost giggle with the rush of the near miss.

"It's done," I say.

Kellogg turns his radio on. It crackles, and the light on top glows green. "A good sign," he says, then holds the radio to his lips. "What do you see?"

Silence for a moment, then a voice says, "I see the moon. I see stars," and the men in the room start screaming at the top of their lungs. It goes on and on, and I can't help but feel the rush. There is starlight. And power.

The director tries to hurl herself into the Black, but enough men are guarding her that she can't. I almost want to let her go through, to let her die. She's too dangerous in our world.

I kneel next to Albin's body. His arm is trapped under his back, and I pull it free and lay it on his chest. "Thank you," I whisper, though I'm not sure why. He didn't help because he thought we were worth saving.

It seems like it takes forever, but eventually we leave the Verge and experience the sky for ourselves. It feels warmer now, even though the sun is hours from rising. Looking up at the moon brings more tears. I allow myself to feel joy for the lives saved, but with it comes pain for the lives lost.

"What have you done?" the director says next to me. Someone was smart enough to wrap a chain around her chest, pinning her arms to her sides.

"Only what you did to us."

She smiles. "We will survive. We know what it is to live without light. Without power."

I find myself encouraged by her words. "I hope that's true. I really do. But we have no idea what the future looks like right now. For all you know, your home is gone."

"I'll find out soon."

"Actually, I don't think you will."

Her lip twitches, but she doesn't ask what I mean. She can find out later that she has no chance of getting back home, that there will never be another war between worlds. That it is truly over.

What that means for me, I have no idea. But I'm excited to find out.

I meet up with the others outside the Verge. There are honest-to-God birds chirping somewhere. It's the middle of winter and there are birds chirping. It's like the whole world is waking up.

Peter is looking at the stars, but then his gaze drops to me, and he smiles. Sophia wraps her arms around me. It feels great. I want her joy to infect me; I want to feel it too.

"You did it," is all she says.

Peter kisses me full on the mouth, then holds me close. "I'm sorry," he says. "I'm proud of you." He knows me; there will be time to talk later.

Noble has a careful smile, like he's trying to keep it in place. A little bit of blood crusts his earlobe. "Well done," he says, before pulling me into a hug. He doesn't let go, and I feel a tremble in his body. He pulls back, wiping at his eye. "When did I turn into a big, crying child?" he says, not really asking.

People are milling about in the park, like they don't know what to do or where to go. They will probably never fully understand what happened here. I'm sure for now they only feel joy as they stare up at the stars, as the lights flicker on in the apartments surrounding the park. They think the future is bright and sunny. They have no idea what darkness awaits us all in the blink of an eye.

To the south I see two Axes coasting above the skyscrapers, and a familiar fear grabs my stomach, but they turn into giant fireballs two seconds later. And two seconds after that, four US military fighter jets scream overhead, spreading out to cover the city. The surviving Roses from the Verge are on their knees, hooded and bound. None of them are stupid enough to use their power now that they've seen the light from the moon. They know it's all over.

Soon the military is everywhere in the city. There are tanks up and down every street. Humvees bounce through the park, their gunners swiveling on top, scanning for any threats. In the distance I can hear people screaming, but not from terror or panic. They're victory screams. A horn blows, and then another. Then the city is full of honking horns. My team sits through it all next to the Verge, soaking it in. Relishing the noises that say we are still here. A van full of men in black combat gear pulls up to us eventually. They get out and ask us some questions. They want us to go with them. That's fine with us. We're done fighting.

The president wants to address the world as soon as possible, a speech that will loop again and again as power is restored across the globe. People in the city are only just starting to realize that the blackout was on a global scale.

We talk about what to do next in a hotel the government has secured for us—one of the few safe buildings in New York. Important civilians are staying here as well, with plans to tour the city in the coming days. They want to get a message out to the nations of the world as quickly as possible. One that says *The US government is most definitely still here, and operational. Don't try anything stupid.*

It's only been a day, but people are already flocking to the city to see the Verge, the first real proof that we are not alone in the multiverse. The government has set up a hundred-yard perimeter around it.

"I don't know," Peter says to me in the hotel lobby. "People won't trust us no matter what. I think we should just disappear."

I'm feeling really good. I've been taking pain pills for my injuries, but I found that if I take one more, I feel extra good. So good it's hard to remember what I did, and hard to feel anything when I do. The director's words keep running through my head—*We will survive. We know what it is to live without light.* I cling to them for comfort.

"The world wants the truth," Noble says, "and we can give it to them. No cover stories. It's over, and there is zero chance of this happening again. The truth will unite us."

"Like when the whole world bands together against an alien threat," Sophia says. We all look at her. "I've been watching movies."

It's funny, but it's true. Our world was on the wrong track, divided. But now? Who knows. The coming months and years will define the rest of our existence. One day, we might even thank True Earth.

"You kids need to make your choice," Noble says. "But keep in mind the world knows our faces already. Or at least yours. You can run and hide for the rest of your lives, or you can address the world as heroes. They'll probably give you medals."

"Like in *Star Wars*," Sophia says.

So we agree to do it. We ride in a convoy down to Washington, D.C. The military has cleared a path through the highways, but there are still abandoned cars everywhere, and the roads aren't fully open to the public yet. There are dead bodies here and there, in a car, in a ditch, in the road. The world's near fall into destruction is apparent everywhere we look, and it will probably be that way for a long time. Maybe forever. How can anything truly go back to normal when people have experienced a taste of the end of the world? We ride to D.C., and Peter holds my hand the entire trip.

But he doesn't look at me.

We do the address inside the White House, since it's not safe outside. Or so a Secret Service agent tells me. Order has not been completely restored. Many cops haven't come back to work yet. The president meets with us in an underground room surrounded by about five hundred agents, where we spend an hour briefing him. He shakes our hands. He reaches me last, leans in, and says, "Thank you," with such sincerity I almost start to cry. I don't want to be thanked. I don't want to be reminded ever again. But I will be. It's my burden to bear.

The president gives us a rundown of what he's going to say and how he's going to introduce us, and then we walk into the press room. Peter's still avoiding my gaze, and I can't figure out why.

The reporters are back to work, that's for sure. We all walk up onto the platform and the flashes start going off and I can't see anything. I actually squint and turn my head.

The president holds his hands up. "No pictures for a moment, please."

Questions are shouted. *Who are they? Where did they come from? Are they from a different universe?*

The president explains True Earth as more flashes go off and we stand there awkwardly in a row next to him. "You are now looking at a team of exiles who fought against the world they came from." Not exactly true, but close enough. "Without them, we would still be in the dark."

He introduces each of us and says some things we've done. He tells the world I stopped the eyeless invasion a few months ago, even though it wasn't just me. He thankfully doesn't mention how I had to kill myself to do it.

The screen behind us shows a tall picture of Rhys. Sophia and I made them do it. People need to see his face, to know what he sacrificed. The picture is one Sophia took in the apartment on Columbus Circle. Rhys is sitting at a table, smiling, a big red Christmas mug in front of him. Steam is rising from the mug. Seeing his smile is a knife to my heart.

We don't have any photos of Noah and Olive, but the president talks about them briefly, presenting them as soldiers who died valiantly in our fight against evil. "They are gone," he says, "but we will not forget them."

The president goes on to explain the most recent attack,

at least as well as he can, then comes back to me and says, "This young lady led a daring siege on the enemy's stronghold. She ended the war, the occupation, and restored daylight and power." There are a million questions, because none of it makes sense from an outside perspective. I mean, the sun was blocked. Cars didn't work, and now they do. But the president doesn't make us answer them. He says that will come later. "Now is a time of thanks," he says. "As we rebuild, I want the world to know their saviors. It is a debt we can never repay."

The reporters aren't happy about the half story, but I don't think I could care even if I tried. I just want Peter to look at me. He finally does, at the end, right before we're marched off the platform. He turns his face to me and smiles, but the smile doesn't touch his eyes. The flashes are so bright they draw my attention to something missing on his face. I'm looking at his purple-blue eyes, and then his chin.

His chin does not have a little white scar.

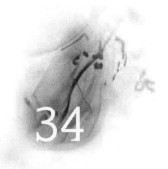

34

My mouth opens. I close it right away, but I saw his eyes flick down. He noticed me noticing. I turn my face toward the cameras and let them take our picture. My heart is pounding so hard I can feel it against my ribs. This white-hot ball of rage inside me just wants to know where Peter is and who this fake person is standing next to me. I'm going to find out.

They thought of every little detail but a scar you can hardly see.

We file off the stage in a line, and I decide it's not too late to recover. I grab the imposter's hand and give it a squeeze, then stand up on my tiptoes to whisper in his ear. "Why don't you come to my room when things settle down?" The president has us staying in the White House—I'm in the Lincoln Bedroom with Sophia, and Peter is in the Queens' Bedroom with Noble, right across the hall.

"How come?" He's kind of smiling.

"Oh, I don't know," I say, trying to make my voice sound playful, which I don't have much practice at. "Maybe I just want to celebrate all of this being over. In private."

He smiles, and now I wonder how I've been so blind. Peter would never smile like that—all slimy and devious.

This was the mole for the director. He told her the attack was coming. My mind rewinds through all the conversations I had with Peter. He was against attacking in the first place.... Was it this imposter all along? Have I never actually seen my Peter since I've been back? No, that's impossible. I remember seeing Peter's scar the first time I saw him in the Verge. Back when we were both pretending to be someone else. The switch had to have been when Albin came for me the first time, when he tricked me into revealing our base in the Time Warner Center. Or maybe after, when I was unconscious for four days. *Where are you, Peter?*

If I can get the imposter to come to my room, I can neutralize him before he can hurt anyone. Then we'll just have to explain to the president what happened. It might ruin some of our goodwill, but there's no other way. I'm not about to sound the alarm and risk this guy using his fear waves on all these people.

Plus there's a part of me that wants to believe there's an

explanation, and a very small part of me that has doubt. I want to see his chin again. I want to see if he has an excuse.

In the East Sitting Hall, Peter and Noble go into their bedroom. Peter looks at me one last time and gives me a real smile that is so much like the Peter I know that I question everything I saw. He could just be acting weird because of all that's happened . . . or because of what I've done. I hadn't considered that possibility—he was never 100 percent on the plan. Maybe he's upset about the choice I made.

Back in our room, Sophia turns to me with bloodshot eyes. "I need a shower, and then a nap, in that order. Is that fine?"

My mouth opens to tell her what I saw—or rather, what I didn't see—but she's already turning away, walking with such heavy shoulders that I don't want to bother her. "Sure," I say. "Go ahead."

Rather than wait for him, I decide to pay Peter a little visit myself. I spend a minute imagining different scenarios and possible reactions from him. One I like, the others end with one or both of us dead.

I open the door to my room quietly, as Sophia starts the shower. Then I tiptoe across the hall to the Queens' Bedroom. The door is cracked, just an inch. I pause, listening hard for any sounds coming from within. I tilt my ear toward the door, and that's why I see the stain on the hall carpet. It's just a few yards away, where the hallway turns to the right. The red carpet is a darker shade there, the stain about the size of a plate. It could be anything—it could be spilled water.

I sidestep toward it, and just around the corner lies the body of a Secret Service agent on his back, throat slashed.

"Oh no."

I kick open the door to the Queens' Bedroom, but it's too late. Noble is on the floor, a halo of blood around his head, both hands clamped on his neck. His eyes roll toward me. Blood bubbles on his lips. I fall to my knees next to him.

"Too late," he says through the blood.

No! I want to be on the other side. I want to be the one looking up, not down. I'm always looking down.

"Let me see," I say, my voice sounding cold and alien.

"Too late," he says again. "Get him."

"I'm going to stay with you." I'm crying again. I thought I wouldn't have to cry anymore.

Noble closes his eyes. "Be safe," he says, and then says no more.

I'm on my feet and through the door, tearing down the hallways as fast as I can run. I grab a gun off a fallen agent who actually managed to draw it before dying. The hallway is filled with the bodies of agents ordered to guard us. I know where Peter is going. The Black. He'll want to go home, or at least try. He knows it's poisoned, but maybe he thinks he can survive the trip through. There's nowhere else for him to go.

I make it to the exit by following the trail of carnage. Outside the sun is so bright it makes my eyes ache. I sprint across the south lawn, past Marine One, toward the Washington Monument straight to the south. My mind is frozen with grief, but it still shows me memories from this place, from when I rode a horse across the grass, trying to stop Nina from ending the entire world. It was night then, and the air was full of machine-gun fire and sirens. Now there are just patches of snow and blue sky and quiet as the world continues its slow awakening.

The hole to the tunnel that leads to the Black was covered up with a small cinder-block hut. Of course the government didn't just seal it—they wanted to study it. The guards in the hut are dead too, throats slashed. My lungs burn from the freezing air, but I can't stop, I have to catch him before he goes through. I sprint down the tunnel on numb legs for what seems like miles. I want to laugh at myself for believing it was over, that we'd won. That we were going to live as one big happy family.

Finally I'm in the giant cavern where I first saw the Black with Peter and Rhys. It's still strewn with huge chunks of the Verge from Gane's world.

And Peter is standing right next to the edge.

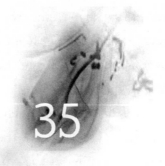

35

"*ON'T MOVE!*" I scream at the top of my lungs, gun leveled at him, the sights over his center mass.

He turns toward me slowly. Blood covers his arms and chest and neck. It's smeared on his face.

"You knew," he says. "I could see the change in your eyes. That's the only reason I did this."

"Where is Peter?"

He raises an eyebrow and smiles grimly. "He did not go quietly, let me tell you."

I can't stop my voice from cracking and shaking. "Tell me where he is or I *swear to God I will end you.*"

"If I told you, I bet you'd shoot me anyway."

"You don't have a choice."

He shrugs. "In that case, your precious boyfriend is in True Earth. The director wanted him secure in case she needed to leverage you once again. You trapped him there. You probably killed him."

I go down on one knee, the air driven out of me. My head hangs, and I don't have the strength to lift it.

I trapped Peter over there. I left him to die. I will never see him again.

The imposter is laughing at me, and I find time to wonder how people like him can exist. How can a human start as a blank slate and then become something like this? I will never understand us. I will never understand any of it.

"How does it feel?" he says. "I must admit, I wish you hadn't noticed who I was. I was ready to live here. With you."

"I would've noticed eventually. It never would've lasted."

"But it was a nice idea. I liked being a hero. And I liked being with you. It could've become real over time."

"Never."

He makes a sound that's almost a laugh. "What gave me away?"

I don't say anything.

"So what happens if I jump through? You poisoned it, right? What happens?"

"You'll have to jump to find out." My voice is shaky and watery and hoarse. "Jump, or I'll shoot you and throw you in."

He looks down at the Black. I fire a shot at his feet, and he flinches away.

"I have nowhere to go," he says.

"Well, maybe you'll survive the trip," I say, knowing he won't. "Jump. Now."

Peter stares at me with this devastated look I will always remember, anguish breaking through for a second. And then he steps forward and falls into the Black, disappearing completely. I know at that moment the Dark Room did its job. The surface of the Black simmers and smokes, and dark particles drift and swirl to the ceiling high above.

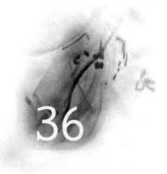

36

It doesn't take them long to find me. I haven't moved, I just curled up on my side on the hard rock floor. I hear the sounds of the soldiers in the tunnels, echoing for two minutes before they reach me. Their boot steps thump along the floor. They surround me with assault rifles.

Kellogg crouches in front of me. "Hey there."

I look up at him.

"Did Peter go through?"

"It wasn't Peter. And yes."

Kellogg nods. "This changes things. You guys are already famous."

"I know." I still haven't moved.

"We have Sophia in custody. She's okay. But we're gonna need you to answer some questions. I can vouch for you." He grabs my cold hand and holds it in his warm one. "I will be with you the whole way. Don't give up yet, okay? Don't shut down."

Slowly, I sit up. Peter wouldn't want me to shut down. He would never want that. Even with what I did to him. Even though I trapped him behind enemy lines, forever.

"There's one thing you can help us with," Kellogg says. "Something that will get you back some trust, I think."

I hug my knees to my chest. The soldiers are still all around us with their guns pointed in my general direction.

"What is it?" I say.

"The director is in custody in a special facility, along with other Roses we've detained. She claims she has vital information for us, but she only wants to talk to you. Can you do that?"

Me?

Why would she want to talk to me?

"Yes," I say. "I can do that."

The director is in a location so secret they have to blindfold me. I don't bother to pay attention to the time and turns—I just let them guide me. I'm cuffed until they lead me through some chilly hallways and into an interview room, which contains a metal table, two chairs, and a one-way mirror.

The director is wearing some kind of helmet, probably to prohibit her fear waves, if that's even possible. It makes her look ridiculous and not scary at all. Her hands are chained to the table, which is welded to the floor.

"What do you want?" I say.

She's straight to business. No more villainous talk. She knows she lost. "If you free me, I will tell you where to find Peter."

Just hearing her speak his name makes my skin crawl. She doesn't deserve to say it. "Peter is trapped in True Earth. Try again."

She shakes her head briskly. "No. He was there briefly, but I had him moved back here at the last minute to use against you."

My heart starts pounding with hope, which is dangerous. I don't want to hope. Not right now. I like the way I feel—I like feeling nothing.

"You're lying."

"What does your heart tell you?"

"I'm not sure I have one left."

"Yes, you did isolate and sentence the future to what you think is a cold death. That would hurt one's heart. But I guess that's my fault, isn't it?" She doesn't seem angry about it any-more, just sad. Introspective, maybe. She must be wondering how it came to this. Beaten by herself.

"I guess."

"Free me and I'll tell you where he is."

"I could never get you out of here alive. You know that."

"I didn't say I wanted to be alive. I said I want to be *free*. I can never go home. So kill me. Kill all the Roses before your world figures out what makes us tick. Don't you see? You haven't won. Unless you do this, they will examine us, experiment on us, and that will lead to one thing—re-creating us."

She's right. As long as we're here, I can't trust anyone to not want what's inside my head. While I'm in this building, I could be in danger. They might never let me leave.

"Do the right thing, Miranda," she says. Her eyes are desperate. She is pleading with me. Pleading with me to end her life.

Who am I to say no?

"Okay. Tell me."

I lean forward and she whispers Peter's location in my ear. Then the door bursts open and men in suits are trying to grab at me, but I'm a Rose and they are not. I reach forward and grab the director's head in both hands and twist as hard as I can. Her neck breaks with a loud pop and her head falls to the table hard. The men carry me out of the room, and I don't resist. But I also can't help but smile.

And hope.

I'm in custody for three days.

On the first day the president himself admitted that the remaining Roses will be kept for further study, and because as a world leader America can't just execute its enemies because they're dangerous (this last part makes me laugh).

There's nothing I can do about it, for now. The Roses will be kept in comas, he assures me. They will pose no danger, he assures me. I can only hope that's true. Kellogg visits me on the second day, and we talk about nothing of relevance until he leans in and whispers, "The Roses mysteriously passed away in the night." Then he looks at me and shrugs. I never see him again.

On day three they release me, but I have to remain under supervision. A dozen agents bring me to Sophia, who was also detained and released, and we hug a long time. Sophia agrees to come with me. To stay with me. We're all each other has right now.

One hour after being freed, I easily lose my guard of agents. I don't even have to hurt them.

The airlines aren't running just yet, but we find a boat that's going across the Atlantic. The captain lets us come aboard if we work, hauling nets full of fish out of the water. The captain and his crew were stranded at sea without power, he tells us, until it mysteriously turned back on. Now it's back to work. Living and working on that boat for a few weeks is the most fun I've ever had. We play cards at night with the crew, and they're totally respectful of us. Sophia smiles again. I laugh again. Because we're going to get Peter. I hold on to that the entire time. The director was many things, but I don't think she would lie to me in the end. Not with what she was asking me to do. She knew I'd see the lie. So I hold on to hope tightly.

We change boats three times, until we're deep in the Mediterranean. The breeze on the water is warm, and then it's cold. The last boat will take us to a tiny island in Greece named Ikaria. A month has passed by the time we make it to the island.

The first week there, Sophia gathers materials to make new memory shots, for the day when we run out of Noble's stockpile and I start forgetting things. I scour the stony beaches and stores, asking people if they've seen someone with Peter's description. Some people say they have, but there are many people here with dark hair. Not many of them have purplish-blue eyes, though.

I know what to expect when I find him. It's the same way he found me, not so long ago.

But it still hurts.

He's working in a café on the beach. It's his break. He's wearing his apron, sitting at a table, drinking coffee from a tiny cup, staring at the waves. The breeze ruffles his hair, which is longer than before and curling at the neck. He spots me and his eyebrows rise like he's surprised to see me. But not because he knows who I am.

He must realize the face he's making, because he quickly drops his gaze and pretends to study the shells at his feet. But then he's looking at me again, out of the corner of his eye. I keep staring. After not seeing him for so long, there's nothing else I can do but stare. I walk over to him slowly, like I'm approaching a wild animal that might bolt at any second.

"Hello," I say.

He smiles up at me. "Hi. You're an American."

"Kind of."

He doesn't say anything. The little patio area is completely empty. He gestures at the seat across from him. "Do you want to sit down?"

"I'd love to," I say, maybe a little too eagerly. But his smile seems happy.

We sit for a moment, just enjoying the breeze and the sound of the waves. He keeps fighting a smile. Finally he says, "This is gonna sound crazy, but you look so completely familiar to me, which is kind of a big deal. Have we met before?"

"We have."

His eyes light up. "Really?" He leans forward. "You know who I am?"

I can feel my eyes tearing up. "I do."

He pauses. "Wait. Then what is my name?"

"Peter," I say without hesitation.

He stares at me, and for a second, even though I know it's not real, I think I see recognition in his eyes. "Do you know how I lost my memory?"

I nod.

"How?"

"It's a long story," I say.

He shakes his head. "I forget things all the time. I forget things each day. I can make a good cup of coffee, thank God, or else I'd be fired. Every morning the owner comes and gets me and tells me what to do. I don't even know if he pays me. I don't know how I got here, or why I have this job. I don't even speak Greek."

Somehow I'm holding both of his hands across the table. I don't remember grabbing them, but now I feel their warmth. His hands are callused from the weapons we used to use. "I can help you remember. This might sound crazy, but we've actually known each other since we were kids. We've been friends for a long time."

His eyes are wet and so are mine. It's like he wants to believe it, but it's too good to be true. He's lived a month or more in confusion, and now it's all going to be over.

"Really? That would be great."

I squeeze his hands.

"So we were friends, huh?" he says.

I try not to smile. "Well, maybe a little more than that. My name is Miranda. Miranda North."

"Pleased to meet you," he says, voice brimming with laughter.

"I have a lot to tell you. A lot. And it's going to be hard to believe. But *you* made me believe it once, and I think I can do that for you. I know I can."

He's shaking his head. "I already believe you. I can't explain it, but I do."

"Good. Then believe this. I'm going to give you a syringe filled with weird liquid, and you're going to inject it into your arm, and then you'll stop forgetting things. When I had this problem, you just jabbed me without asking, but I'm nicer than you."

He laughs. "I believe that too."

"Do you want to go for a walk?"

"On the beach?" He looks at the waves. "Okay." He rises, taking off his apron. He calls toward the kitchen. "Hey, guy! I'm leaving!"

His boss comes out, then looks at me, throws up his hands, and goes back inside.

"Is his name Guy? Or do you just call him that?"

"I don't know what his name is," Peter says, then laughs

again. He takes the syringe that Sophia filled and sticks it in his arm without looking, like he's done it a thousand times, which he has.

I start laughing too, fighting back tears. I don't want to blur my vision.

I want to keep seeing him clearly.

"Okay, a walk. And then what?" he says.

"Whatever we want. We have the rest of our lives." We finally have the rest of our lives.

Peter holds out his hand. "I like the sound of that."

ACKNOWLEDGMENTS

I could not have done this alone in any universe. Thank you to everyone at New Leaf: Suzie Townsend, Joanna Volpe, Danielle Barthel, Pouya Shahbazian, Jackie Lindert, Jaida Temperly, and Dave Caccavo. The usual suspects.

Thank you to Catherine Onder and Lisa Yoskowitz. The work you guys have done on this series is nothing short of incredible. I've learned so much from both of you.

Thank you to: everyone at Hyperion for making my dreams come true. Dana Kaye and everyone at Kaye Publicity. Janet Reid.

Moral support: Adam "I see Don creepin in bay 4" Lastoria, Will "12JX-WATERHAWK" Lyle, and Dan "Backpack"

Lastoria. Susan Dennard and Sarah Maas (GDC4Lyfe). My parents and siblings. Joe Volpe, for growing the beard I cannot. Travis and Barbara Poelle, and sad fat dragons everywhere. Sean Ferrell and Jeff Somers, bastards. Brooks Sherman and Adam Silvera. Whitney Ross and Corey Whaley.

And finally but most importantly, thank you. Thanks for reading. The only reason this story exists outside of my mind is because you read it. That's a gift I can't describe.